The MAGICAL
LAND of NOOM

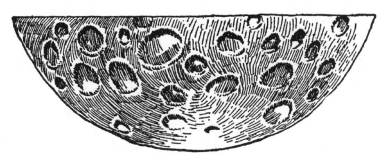

D1501099

The MAGICAL LAND of NOOM

by
JOHNNY GRUELLE

with
Sundry and Mondry
Illustrations
by the Author

ECHO POINT BOOKS & MEDIA, LLC

First publication, 1922

Introduction © Echo Point Books & Media

ISBN: 978-1-62654-984-5

Published by Echo Point Books & Media
www.EchoPointBooks.com

Printed in the U.S.A.

Down, down, the Slide Raft sped,
until it was going so fast that its occupants could not talk.

INTRODUCTION

Best known as the creator of Raggedy Ann and Andy, Johnny Gruelle started his career as a newspaper cartoonist, later to become the author of a number of children's books. Gruelle was born in Arcola, Illinois in 1880. His father was a multi-talented artist who inspired Gruelle's own passion for visual art.

Gruelle's career began in 1903 when he was hired as the assistant illustrator of the new *Indianapolis Star*. As his talent was recognized, other papers sought Gruelle to draw political cartoons.

In 1910 he entered his comic *Mr. Twee Deedle* in the *New York Herald's* drawing contest and won. In addition to the two-thousand dollar prize, the *Herald* offered Gruelle a contract to draw a weekly full-color page. Gruelle's work continued to expand to other newspapers, but focused on cartoons for children. His work became so popular with children, he is credited with playing an important role in increasing newspaper circulation throughout the country, and newspapers added cartoons for kids as a regular feature (previously newspaper cartoons tended to only be political).

As his renown grew, Gruelle began extensive work for a variety of magazines. He also began illustrating children's books, the first of which was a lavishly illustrated edition of *Grimms' Fairy Tales*. In 1916 Gruelle found his book-publishing home with P. F. Volland. His first book for Volland was as the illustrator for Rose Strong Hubbell's *Quacky Doodles' and Danny Daddles' Book*. Two years later, modeled after his daughter's treasured rag doll, Gruelle's *Raggedy Ann Stories* debuted. Readers found the doll as loveable as did his daughter, and her adventures (along with brother Andy) found a huge following. A series of Raggedy Ann and Andy stories and merchandise followed.

The success of the Raggedy Ann series led Gruelle to author a variety of children's books. Intrigued by the creativity and commercial success of L. Frank Baum's *Wizard of Oz* series, Gruelle created *The Magical Land of Noom*. In *The Magical Land of Noom*, Johnny and Janey embark on a fantastical adventure in their flying machine, reaching the far side of the moon. Although *The Magical Land of Noom* never gained the enormous popularity of the Raggedy Ann and Andy series, it is arguably one of Gruelle's finest and most unforgettable works, sought after by collectors and passed on from generation to generation. Gruelle's exquisite watercolor panels and whimsical pen-and-ink drawings match its enchanting plot and quirky collection of characters.

CONTENTS

ILLUSTRATIONS

CHAPTER I

Johnny and Janey Fly Away to the Moon

GRAN'PA had finished building the chicken coop and he walked out in front of the house to speak to a neighbor.

Johnny and Janey, who had been watching Gran'pa with such interest, grew tired of waiting for his return.

"Let's build a Flying Machine," Johnny said after a while. "Grand'pa has finished and will not need the boards that are left and we can find plenty of nails."

"Do you think we can build a Flying Machine?" asked Janey, delighted at the idea.

"Easily!" Johnny told her. "Of course we can't make one that will really fly, but we can pretend that it goes 'way up in the air."

"It will be loads of fun!" cried Janey, and she jumped up and down and smiled.

So Johnny got an old box and nailed four or five boards to the sides for wings.

"It should have a sail," Janey said.

"Yes, it needs a sail and a mast and a rudder," replied Johnny. "Run in and ask Gran'ma for an old sheet to make the sail of, will you, Janey? I'll be putting on a mast and the rudder."

When Janey came running back with an old sheet she cried, "I just thought! We must have something to start and stop the Flying Machine with, so Gran'ma gave me two empty spools. We can use them."

"Just the thing!" Johnny answered. "I'll put them at the front of the box and label one 'Start' and the other 'Stop.'"

"How can we guide the Flying Machine when we get to flying?" Janey asked. "When we make believe we're flying, I mean."

"I've put only one nail in the rudder," Johnny replied, "so that by pulling on these strings we can guide it. See?" And Johnny showed his sister how the board with only one nail in it turned from side to side as he pulled the strings.

"Oh! That's fine!" Janey exclaimed. "I'll ask Gran'ma if we may have some lunch to take with us on our trip," she added, as she ran into the house.

When Janey came out with a tiny basket of lunch Johnny had marked "Polly Ann" on both sides of the box. He had fastened the sail made from the old sheet to a stick and run a string through a screw-eye, so that the sail could be raised or lowered whenever they might wish.

"Let's see!" Johnny mused. "Have we everything we need?"

"Well, here are the wings, the rudder, the 'Start' and 'Stop' spools and the sail," Janey told him. "I think that is all, don't you?"

"All right, then, Sis! Put the lunch on one of the sails. No!" and Johnny hammered a nail on one side of the box, "hang the basket of lunch there and climb in. It's going to be a tight squeeze for both of us. But it won't take this Flying Machine long to get to Mars or Venus or the Moon, and we can get out and rest on some of the Stars if we get tired."

"Let's go to the Moon first, and then to the Milky Way!" Janey cried.

"All right, if you are ready!" Johnny agreed, as he sat in the bottom of the box, in front of Janey. "Hold your hat, Sis, for here she goes!"

And Johnny turned one of the spools in the front of the box.

"Oh! isn't the view grand from up here, Johnny!" Janey cried. "See, there is Gran'ma's house 'way down below, and we are getting closer to the Moon all the time!"

"Those are queer birds flying by, Sis," said Johnny, who could make believe any way he liked. "Can you make out what they are?"

"Yes," Janey answered, as she looked at the chickens in the yard, "they are Eagles. See that beautiful big one with the red comb? That's a Roc!"

"My, I wish this Flying Machine would really Fly!" Johnny said, a little later. "But it's fun pretending anyway. Let's get out at the next Star, Sis, and eat our lunch. I didn't eat much breakfast and I'm hungry!"

"All right, Brud!" said Janey, who wasn't tired of the play either. "Wait a minute!" as Johnny started to climb out of the box. "You forgot to stop the Flying Machine."

"Well, I'll bring it to a stop very slowly," Johnny told her. "So that we won't strike these mountain-tops and tip over!"

And he turned the "Stop" spool a fraction of an inch.

Neither of the children was prepared for what followed.

The Polly Ann shot up over the fence, suddenly, scattering the startled chickens in all directions, and as Johnny and Janey crouched low in the box the familiar objects about the farm whizzed by them like bullets.

"We are really going!" Janey gasped, as they sped upward. "I feel as if I'd like to jump!"

At this Johnny caught his sister's foot and held it tight.

"Don't look over the side until you get used to flying!" he cautioned her, very wisely.

"Twist the other spool!" Janey told him. "I don't like to be up so high. Everything seems so small."

Johnny gave the other spool a twist and the Flying Machine swept ahead at twice its former speed.

"You're twisting the wrong spool!" Janey screamed.

"You must have been twisting the wrong one all the time, somehow. See, you've been twisting the one marked 'Start.'"

"Sure enough! That's just what I did," Johnny admitted. "Well, I'll twist the other now."

The Flying Machine came to such a sudden halt that the children were almost thrown from the box, and the basket of lunch was whirled off its nail so suddenly that it flew straight ahead of the Flying Machine for nearly a hundred feet before it curved to the earth.

The children watched it curve and circle as it fell. Then the paper came off and there was a regular shower of sandwiches, doughnuts and small cakes.

"Now, Mister! You be careful or we'll never get back!" Janey cried as she clutched her brother tightly by the collar. "Send the Flying Machine down to the ground again, Johnny. Please do!"

But the Flying Machine, when it stopped, hung suspended in the air although when Johnny gently twisted the "Start" spool and it started off again, it went in the opposite direction from the earth.

"It won't go down," cried Johnny, as he brought the Flying Machine to a stop again. "What shall we do?"

'Well, if it won't go down, there's nothing to do but go on!" Janey answered. "It's all your fault for building the Flying Machine!"

"Now, Sis, that isn't fair!" cried Johnny. "You know

you suggested putting on the spools, and if we'd left them off we shouldn't have started. What we should have thought of was something to make the Flying Machine go up or down as we wanted. Now it only goes ahead or stops."

"Try guiding it with the rudder," Janey suggested.

So Johnny twisted the "Start" spool, and as the Flying Machine started forward he pulled one of the rudder strings. The Flying Machine slowly turned and flew in a large circle.

"We can't do it!" Janey cried, the tears coming to her eyes. "We can't make it go down as we want to! We're only flying in a circle above Gran'ma's farm. See! Gran'ma and Gran'pa and a lot of other people are out looking at us!"

Sure enough, so far below that they looked like tiny specks of dust, the children could see their grandparents and many of the neighbors watching them as they sailed.

Johnny brought the Flying Machine to a stop directly over Gran'ma and Gran'pa and the neighbors, and they could hear Gran'pa calling to them quite distinctly. The children called back at the top of their voices, but they couldn't make Gran'ma and Gran'pa hear.

Johnny tried twisting first one spool and then the other, but this jerked the Flying Machine so violently that his sister objected. She said she would rather go on than stay just where they were, doing nothing. So the children took off their hats and waved farewell to the people below, and Johnny, twisting the "Start" spool gently at first, increased the speed until the Flying Machine sped along like a meteor, leaving the farm far below and behind.

The different colors in the fields gave the Earth a sort of patchwork effect, but as the Flying Machine climbed higher and higher the yellows and greens and blues blended together until the Earth was more the color of an opal. In fact, the children now saw a continuous change of colors, ranging from a deep yellow to a bluish purple, with every now and then a speck of crimson as the sunlight glanced along a hill.

"Isn't it beautiful!" Janey cried. "I don't feel as if I wished to jump any more, do you, Brud?"

"No, I don't feel like jumping," her brother answered, and he stopped the Flying Machine so that he could see better. "Look, Sis, what causes that yellow blaze down there?"

They both looked over the side of the Flying Machine and saw the Earth bathed in a sheen of gold, with here and there glimpses of brilliant purple showing.

"Oh! I know what it is now!" Janey cried, presently. "A thunder storm has just passed between us and the Earth and the sun is shining on the Clouds. Look! See the lightning?"

A faint rumble came up to them as of someone rolling potatoes down a wooden trough, and a vivid streak of blue zig-zagged through the yellow of the clouds.

"The purple we see is the Earth in shadow beneath the clouds," Johnny concluded, after a while.

The children watched the strange sight for a long time

before they decided to go on. Then they looked away for a moment, and when they looked back toward the Earth they could not find it at once. They had traveled so far that the Earth now seemed no larger than a bright Star, and but for the fact that it was almost beneath them they would never have recognized it at all.

Lots of other Stars could be plainly seen now. The Moon had grown to an enormous size; in fact, it almost filled the sky behind them. The children were greatly surprised to see it. They had been watching the Stars in front of them and they had not once turned their heads the other way.

"What is that?" Janey cried suddenly, as she grasped her brother's arm and pulled one of the rudder strings so that the Flying Machine swung around to face the Moon.

Johnny was so startled at the wonderful sight that he gave the "Stop" spool a twist and brought the Flying Machine to a stop with a jerk.

"It must be the Moon!" said Johnny, in an awed voice, after he had looked at the enormous object in speechless amazement for fully five minutes.

"It *is* the Moon, Brud!" Janey agreed. "See, there is the Man in the Moon's face as plain as day, and there are mountains and valleys, too. See?"

The Moon, seen from where the children viewed it, was of a pale bluish-greenish tint, except where the rays of the Sun slanted across the mountain peaks and into the deep valleys. It seemed to Johnny and Janey as though they were looking through beautiful blue-green glass down into a dark well; for wherever the Sun did not shine or was not reflected from the mountains into the valleys the Moon's surface was black—so black that it made the rest of the Moon seem transparent. This seemed to the children very strange.

"Say, Sis," Johnny exclaimed, "this can't be the Moon after all! It must be some extra big Star."

"I believe it is the Moon," said his sister, "for, you can

see the face of the Man in the Moon quite plainly. But it is a great deal larger than it usually is, and it doesn't look quite as it does from the earth. But see! There are the Man's eyes and nose and mouth."

"Yes, I see now," Johnny admitted. "But it isn't exactly the same view we have from the Earth."

"You are right, Johnny!" said Janey, after a moment. "It isn't the same view. We must have passed to the other side of the Moon!"

Johnny started the Flying Machine again and steered it toward the Moon. And as they whirled around the side of the Moon the part that resembled a man's face twisted about until it disappeared.

"I can't tell whether we are getting closer to the Moon or not!" cried Johnny anxiously.

Presently, however, they saw the face of the Man in the Moon coming around from the other side.

"We must have made a complete circuit of the Moon," Janey decided. "See, Johnny, the rudder is pulled over to one side! That's the reason!"

Johnny pulled the rudder string until the Flying Machine was aimed right at the Moon, and they approached it at great speed.

"Slow up, Johnny!" Janey cried, when they could make out all the mountain tops and valleys very distinctly. "It feels too much as if we were falling when we go so fast."

So Johnny twisted the "Start" spool backwards until they were flying very slowly and seemed to be floating down toward the Moon's surface as lightly as a feather.

The Flying Machine still was headed directly toward the Moon, and this gave the children the impression that they

were falling. But Johnny, by pulling the rudder about occasionally, steered the Flying Machine so that they landed among large mushrooms and queer ferns, instead of on the mountain tops or in the deep valleys they had seen on the other side of the Moon.

For, although the children did not know this, they had passed around the side of the Moon that always faces the Earth and had alighted in the Magical Land of Noom.

CHAPTER II

Johnny and Janey Meet the Strange Man

BY TWISTING the "Start" spool backward and forward Johnny had brought the Flying Machine to the Moon's surface very gently, but by no twisting of rudder or the spools could he effect a landing except by heading the Flying Machine directly for the surface. It was in this manner that the machine came to rest, with the front of the box resting upon the surface of the Moon, and the rudder sticking up in the air. The children sat in the box as though they were tied there and were very much surprised to find that they did not fall to the ground.

There they sat—directly facing the ground, with their backs to the sky.

"Let's get out and look around, Janey! This feels too funny, sitting this way!" And Johnny started to put his foot over the side of the box down to the Moon.

"Wait a moment!" Janey cried as she caught her brother and held him. "We may tumble back into the sky if we get out of the Flying Machine!"

"I do not think we shall do that! I had not thought of it, though!" Johnny mused.

"One thing certain—it is a long fall to the farm."

Finally Janey cried, "I have it!" And she took off her slipper and held it out to the side of the box. Johnny watched her with much interest.

"If the slipper falls to the ground, it is safe for us to get out!" she said as she dropped it.

The slipper dropped very slowly to the ground.

"It didn't seem to want to go very much!" she said.

"Try the other one," Johnny suggested.

The second slipper floated to the ground in the same manner, very slowly.

This puzzled the children, and they were undecided just what to do until another idea struck Janey. "I'll hold your hand while you climb out, so that if you start to fall up in the air, I can pull you back into the box!" she said.

So while his sister held his hand Johnny stepped from the box to the surface of the Moon and straightened up. "Dear me!" he exclaimed. "You look funny sitting there, Janey. Climb out!"

"How does it feel when you stand up, Johnny?" she asked.

"Natural!" he replied. "Come on!"

"I don't like to!" Janey said, holding to the sides of the box. "It seems so queer."

At this Johnny pushed on the rudder of the Flying Machine and tipped the box over backward, so that his sister found herself sitting up in the box, while the box rested in a natural position upon the ground.

"Oh!" Janey exclaimed, as she stood up beside Johnny. "What a relief! My legs are stiff and cramped."

When she stepped from the box Janey intended hopping up and down to straighten out the cramps, but when she jumped she rose in the air six or eight feet, and Johnny, springing to catch his sister, who seemed about to fly off the Moon, gave such a spring he rose ten feet in the air and passed her.

Both children settled slowly to the ground, and when they reached there they sat down and held to mushrooms.

Johnny wiped the perspiration from his forehead. "My goodness! I thought we were both goners then," he said.

Presently they both laughed. "How silly we are! If we had only thought we wouldn't have been scared a bit!"

Johnny exclaimed. "The Moon is so much lighter than the earth the attraction of gravity is not so strong, and we naturally are lighter. Look at this, Sis!" he continued jumping up in the air and throwing his feet out in front of him, so that he took what in the water is called "A Seat in Congress."

"Be careful, Bud!" Janey exclaimed anxiously.

"We are safe," said Johnny as he settled slowly to the ground, "and we can have barrels of fun doing stunts! Whee!" and he stamped both feet upon the ground and gave such a spring that he turned over and over in the air four or five times before he settled to the ground again.

Janey could not see so much fun without being in it herself, so she caught Johnny's hand and they turned flip-flops and jumped up into the air and pretended they were swimming as they came down. They were having the best time of their lives.

Then, seeing some giant mushrooms not far off, Johnny called to Janey and ran toward them. When about twenty feet away he leaped and sailed through the air up to the top of the tallest, one about ten feet high. Janey followed, and they jumped from one mushroom to another. Sometimes they missed the jump, but this did not matter, as they settled to the ground easily and gently.

Janey and Johnny played among the giant mushrooms for a long time, doing all sorts of tricks, and jumping around until they grew tired.

As they sat under an immense fern, resting, Johnny said, "It's too bad we lost the lunch, Sis. I'm beginning to feel hungry!"

"I should like some of Granny's doughnuts!" Janey said. "Let's see if we can find any berries or fruit to eat. I've read that is the way all shipwrecked people do."

"Perhaps we shall have to live on mussels and clams," said Johnny as he. arose. "Let's find something! I could almost eat one of these mushrooms!" And Johnny broke off a piece of mushroom and held it towards Janey.

Janey caught a whiff of the mushroom and said, "It smells good enough to eat!"

Johnny smelt the piece he had in his hands and then took a tiny bite.

"Be careful, Johnny!" Janey warned. "You know Granny said there was really no way to tell whether a mushroom was a mushroom or a toad-stool, except by eating it, and if you ate it and it was poison it was a toad-stool, and if you ate it and it did not hurt you, it was a mushroom!"

"Ummmmm!" Johnny exclaimed, when he had tasted the mushroom. "It's fine, Janey!" and Johnny broke off another piece and ate it as if it had been cake.

"I'll wait and see if it poisons you first!" said Janey.

Johnny picked off pieces of different mushrooms and tried them. "They're different, Janey!" he cried. "You're missing it! Try this piece! It tastes of raspberry or blackberry, I can't tell which!"

Janey nibbled at the piece Johnny gave her and found the flavor excellent. She went to the mushroom from which Johnny had broken the piece and tore off a chunk as large as her head and began to eat it. The mushrooms were sweet and of different flavors, tasting just like cake. The children discovered that the old mushrooms which had turned brown were of chocolate or ginger flavor.

"We can't starve with all these goodies!" cried Johnny. "I feel as if I had just finished a Thanksgiving dinner!"

Janey left Johnny sitting under one of the mushrooms and walked about to see if she could discover a spring, as the sweet mushrooms had made her very thirsty.

Johnny had eaten so much it made him drowsy, and before Janey had gone far he was sound asleep.

Janey passed under the mushrooms and giant ferns until she came to an open space in the center of which a spring bubbled up.

Walking up to the spring, Janey was surprised to see no outlet for the water. It bubbled up just as water would bubble in a kettle when boiling, but this water felt very cold when she put her finger in it.

Upon tasting the water Janey found it sour. "Lemonade!" she cried, and running to the side of the clearing she picked a large leaf and folded it for a cup.

The lemonade was just sweet enough, and Janey drank two large leavesful. She was dipping in again when she heard a tread upon the grass behind her.

"Oh, Johnny," she cried, "I've found a spring of lemonade and it is lovely!"

Then, as Johnny did not answer, she turned her head and saw a strange Man approaching her with upraised stick and a fierce frown upon his face.

"Who said you might drink of my spring!" he shouted, quickening his walk to a hop and waving his arms in a threatening manner.

"I—I—I—did not know it was your spring!" the little girl answered, as she scrambled to her feet and dropped her leaf-cup.

"Of course you didn't!" the Strange Man cried as he came up to her and caught her arm fiercely. "Of course you didn't! Of course you didn't!"

And with that he raised his stick above his head as if to strike her. "I'll teach you to drink of my spring!"

Janey screamed and pulled with all her might to get away, but the Strange Man held her tightly.

Johnny, hearing his sister's cry, came running through the ferns, and seeing the Strange Man about to hit Janey, he flew at him like a little tiger. When about eight feet from the Strange Man, Johnny, who was running at good speed, jumped through the air and landed upon the Strange Man's back. The force of his dive carried himself and the Strange Man head over heels, knocked off the Strange Man's tall hat and made him lose his hold upon Janey and the stick.

Johnny was on top when they finally quit rolling and with all his might he pummeled the Strange Man about the head. The Strange Man's long legs kicked through the air and he scratched at Johnny's face with his long fingers.

The Strange Man cried out for Johnny to quit, but Johnny, angry at the Strange Man's treatment of his sister, managed to get his knees on the Strange Man's arms, sat upon his chest and pounded him right and left.

"You just wait! I'll catch you and pay you back!"

"Say enough!" Johnny yelled. "Say enough! Say enough!" and Johnny caught hold of the Strange Man's long hair and bumped his head upon the ground.

Janey held her breath. It was the first time she had ever seen Johnny in a fight, for he was a quiet little fellow and always avoided a fight if it were possible. But now Johnny was very angry, and Janey felt sorry for the Strange Man.

"Let him up, Johnny! He's had enough! He says for you to quit! Let him up!" Janey cried.

"Now, you keep back, Sis!" Johnny shouted, his eyes full of tears. "I'll teach him to strike you! There!—There! Will you ever— There!—do it again?"

"No, I won't! Honest!" the Strange Man cried, closing his eyes tight each time Johnny bumped his head on the ground.

"All right!" Johnny said as he got off of the Strange Man and stood back to see what he would do upon getting up from the ground.

The Strange Man picked up his hat and stick without looking at Johnny, turned and walked across the clearing. When he had reached the other side he looked over his shoulder, and shaking his stick at the children he cried, "You just wait! I'll catch you and pay you back! You just wait!"

Johnny, in spite of his sister's attempt to hold him back, ran across the clearing after the Strange Man, who turned again and sped through the ferns like a deer.

When Johnny reached the edge of the clearing he stamped his feet upon the ground loudly. The Strange Man, thinking Johnny was close behind him, redoubled his efforts and catching his foot in a vine went sprawling among the ferns.

Johnny doubled up with laughter and Janey could not help joining in.

"My! You surely can fight, Johnny!" she said admiringly. Janey put her arm around her brother's neck and kissed him.

"Ah shucks!" said Johnny, embarrassed, "I couldn't stand to see him strike you Janey, but I don't like to fight!"

"Weren't you mad though! You cried!" Janey went on.

"That's it!" Johnny exclaimed. "I get too angry and have to cry like a boo baby! That's why I always get licked, because my eyes fill up with tears and I can't see!"

"Oh Johnny, I'll bet you don't always get licked, either! You can lick anyone I'll bet, if you want to!" his sister said proudly.

"Well of course I really don't get licked every time!" Johnny admitted. Then, with a laugh, he added, "Because sometimes I can run faster than the other fellow and he doesn't catch me!"

"Of course it's wrong to fight!" Janey said as they walked away in a different direction from the one taken by the Strange Man. "It always seems so useless, doesn't it?"

"Unless it's something like this fight!" Johnny answered.

"I guess I couldn't have fought so well if I hadn't been fighting for you! Did he hurt you much, Janey?"

"He hurt me when he pinched my arm, but he didn't hit me with the stick," Janey said, as she showed Johnny the bruised place on her arm.

"It's a good thing I didn't know of that bruise," cried Johnny, "while I had him down!"

As they talked the children came to a path. They walked down it until they saw a queer little house made of sticks plastered together with mud and colored clay.

"What a queer house!" the children cried. "Isn't it small!"

They walked up to the door and knocked. "Come in!" a voice called to them from within.

So the children, pushing open the door, stepped inside.

At first they could see nothing, for the door had swung shut behind them, but presently their eyes growing accustomed to the darkness, they made out a form across the room.

"My! It's dark!" Janey exclaimed. "Can't we have a light!"

The form across the room chuckled and Johnny reached behind him for the door-knob, so that he could let some light into the room. The door was locked!

When Johnny found this out he stepped in front of Janey. "Keep behind me, Sis!" he whispered. "This doesn't seem safe!"

At this moment something struck Johnny in the face and splashed all over. It took him so by surprise he staggered backward and stumbled over Janey, so that both the children fell to the floor.

As he scrambled to his feet Johnny felt his arms caught and a rope whirled around and around his arms and legs, so that he could not move.

A bright flame shot up from the fireplace and the children saw the Strange Man sitting there with a book across his knees. He had just thrown a powder in the fireplace and it burnt brightly.

The Strange Man was the only one in the room except the children and he mumbled to himself as he read from the great book. Johnny looked at Janey and saw that she was tied in much the same manner as himself.

"It's the man who owns the Lemonade Spring," cried Janey.

"Say!" Johnny shouted. "You untie us and let us go, or we'll have you arrested when we get out!"

"You won't get out!" the Strange Man told him. "I'll see to that!"

"Help!" Johnny shouted at the top of his voice, Janey joining him.

"Dear me!" the Strange Man exclaimed fretfully. "How can you expect me to change you into animals when you make so much noise? You distract my mind from my reading, and I am trying to find just how to work the magic!"

"Is that a magic book?" Janey asked.

"Of course!" the Strange Man replied. "And I have to memorize the magic song that I must sing when I puff the magic powder over you and change you into animals, and I can not think when you make so much noise!"

"We're sorry we drank your lemonade!" Janey said.

"I'm sorry I had a fight with you!" Johnny said.

"Yes! I know you are," the Strange Man cried, shaking his stick at them, "and I told you that I would get even with you! I am about to change you into pigs!"

"Oh dear! I don't care to be changed into a pig!" Janey cried.

"I don't believe he can do it!" Johnny told her.

"Oh, don't you!" the Strange Man hissed, as he put down the large book and came towards Johnny. "I can easily change you into a cat, but I am learning the rhyme to change you into pigs and then I'll show you!"

Janey began crying and Johnny said, "Don't cry, Sis!

He's trying to fool you! He can't change us into anything, it isn't possible!"

The Strange Man puffed some powder from a tiny bellows upon Johnny and began to sing.

"A diddle daddle hunka dee, A chunka lunka diddle fee,
  Kerlike kerlunk kachunkapat, and so I change you to a cat!"

"There! I guess you believe it possible now, don't you?" the Strange Man said when he stopped singing.

"Meow!" said Johnny. "Meow!" He *had* changed into a cat.

"Killikaluka, willyculoosa! Now I change you to a boy!" said the Strange Man, again puffing the powder upon Johnny, and changing him back to a boy.

"What shall we do?" Janey cried.

"You must keep still," the Strange Man commanded, "or I can never change you to pigs!"

"Let us keep yelling at the top of our lungs," cried Johnny, "so that he can not study the rhyme to change us into pigs!"

So the two children began yelling at the top of their voices, and the Strange Man grew so impatient he finally said, "Well, if you continue like that, I shall have to go outside and study, but it will be all the worse for you when I do change you to pigs, for I shan't let you see a mud puddle for two years!"

And as the children continued their cries, the Strange Man closed his book and went out by a back door. He stamped along the walk kicking the loose pebbles viciously.

CHAPTER III

Gran'ma and Gran'pa Fly After the Children

WHEN Gran'pa and Gran'ma saw the children fly over the fence they could scarcely believe their eyes. They shouted as loudly as possible for Janey and Johnny to come back.

And when the children circled above the farm in their home-made Flying Machine, all the neighbors, hearing the cries of the two old people, came running over to the farm and watched the strange sight.

When the home-made Flying Machine rapidly disappeared in the sky the two old people put their arms around each other and wept like children.

Of course there was nothing they could do, so they went into the house and sat down upon the old couch.

"They were such good children!" Gran'ma sobbed.

"They were always good children!" Gran'pa cried. "Oh dear! Oh dear!"

All the rest of the day the old people thought of Janey and Johnny and wondered what had become of them.

"I wish we could go in search of them!" Gran'pa said.

"Where did they get such a wonderful Flying Machine?" Gran'ma asked as she wiped the tears from Gran'pa's eyes and her own with her apron.

"They made it from an old box and some boards I had left after finishing my chicken coop!" Gran'pa told her.

"Yes, I remember now!" Gran'ma said. "Janey came in and asked me for an old sheet for a sail, and for two spools. The spools, she said, would be the 'Start' and 'Stop' twisters for the flying machine!"

"It's funny they didn't come back when we called to them!" Gran'pa mused. "They always have minded so well!"

"I don't believe they knew how to work the Flying Machine so that they could return to the earth!" Gran'ma replied. "Perhaps they did not think it would really fly and so neglected to put something on to send the machine down. I am sure that must have been the reason!"

"It must have been!" Gran'pa mused. "But see here, why can't we go after them and bring them back,

Gran'ma! If the children could build a Flying Machine, I see no reason why I couldn't build one! In fact," Gran'pa continued, "I could build a better one, I'm sure!"

"But how do we know where they have gone to?" Gran'ma asked.

"We can easily find out!" Gran'pa said, as he walked to the door. "I will build my machine with many spools on it, and one spool we will mark 'Direction taken by the children' and the machine will follow them everywhere they have gone until we find them! The other spools can be labeled 'Stop,' 'Go,' 'Rise,' 'Lower,' and anything else we can think of. We must be careful and have everything complete before we start!"

"It is six o'clock now," Gran'pa added. "I should have it finished by eight or nine o'clock and we can start the first thing in the morning!"

So Gran'pa took all his tools out in the back yard and began to work.

Johnny had picked out the largest box around the place and all that Gran'pa could find were four little soap boxes; these he nailed together.

A neighbor boy came over to watch Gran'pa, and when he heard what Gran'pa was building he said, "Gran'pa, why don't you borrow my boat? I should be glad to let you have it, and you could put a sail on it and fix it up fine!"

"That will be great, Eddie!" Gran'pa said, "I'll come right over and get it!"

So Gran'pa hitched up old Ned, and telling Gran'ma where he was going, he drove over to Eddie's home and brought back the boat.

It did not take Gran'pa long to make the wings on either side of the boat. He took all the spools he could find and nailed them around the front part. He made a rudder behind that could be turned in any direction. Gran'pa, when he had the boat completed, sat and thought a minute, then he went into the buggy shed and taking two lamps from an old surrey he trimmed the wicks, filled them with oil and fastened them on the sides of the boat.

When he had everything to his liking, it was still daylight and he called Gran'ma to come out and see the new Flying Boat.

"Do you think it will really go?" Gran'ma asked.

"Jump in and let's try it!" Gran'pa cried.

So the two old people climbed into the boat and Gran'pa twisted one of the spools. The Flying Boat rose quietly in the air and flew about as Gran'pa twisted the spools or the rudder.

"It is a success!" both cried as Gran'pa brought the boat back to the starting point.

When they settled to the ground, Gran'ma ran into the house and came out with Gran'pa's coat and hat. She had put on her best bonnet and shawl. She had Janey's and Johnny's coats and several sweaters with her.

Gran'ma had prepared a large basket of food while Gran'pa had been working on the boat, so she told Gran'pa to get this while she filled a jar with water.

"If we find them, the dears will be hungry and thirsty," Gran'ma said, "and it is such a beautiful evening we might as well start now."

"You are right!" Gran'pa exclaimed. "We will start immediately!"

Eddie had remained at home to eat his supper when Gran'pa went for the boat, and now he came running over just in time to see the Flying Boat rise from the ground and go sailing over the fences and trees.

"I'll take care of your place until you come back!" he yelled.

And Gran'pa and Gran'ma, increasing the speed of the Flying Boat, were soon only a speck in the sky.

When they had reached a great altitude, Gran'pa twisted the spool marked "Direction taken by the children" and the Flying Boat swooped down towards the earth until it was on a plane with the course taken by Janey and Johnny; then, as Gran'pa twisted the "Speed" spool, the Flying Boat whizzed through the air so fast that the wind screamed as it rushed in and out of the chinks in the wing boards. Gran'pa and Gran'ma saw the sun rise as they flew over the horizon. The side of the earth away from the sun was in darkness, so that when they flew higher it took on the appearance of a half moon.

Gran'pa looked at his watch and said it was ten-thirty.

"You take a wink of sleep, Gran'ma," he said. "I'll keep watch!"

So Gran'ma rolled up in the blankets she had placed in the boat and was soon fast asleep.

Gran'pa awakened her in about an hour to look at the Moon, which they were approaching at great speed.

"They must have gone to the Moon!" Gran'ma cried. "No, they must have changed their course!" she added after a moment as the Flying Boat, following the course taken by the children, made the circuit of the Moon.

But the Flying Boat soon flew directly at the Moon and the old folks knew the children must have made a landing there.

In fact, the Flying Boat soon landed near the Flying Machine that Johnny had made.

"Here we are!" Gran'pa cried, as he helped Gran'ma from the Flying Boat. "See where they have been sitting in the grass!"

And Gran'ma and Gran'pa followed the children's path in the grass until they came to the spring. There they saw the signs of Johnny's fight.

"It looks as though a struggle had taken place here!" cried Gran'pa.

"Oh! Maybe wild beasts have eaten them up!" cried Gran'ma.

"No! There are no signs of wild beasts!" Gran'pa replied. "We should see their torn clothes about if that were the case! See, their trail leads off this way!"

Gran'pa and Gran'ma at last came to the tiny house of sticks and mud and heard the cries of the children inside.

"Here we are!" Gran'pa cried as he ran around the house.

Gran'ma, lifting her skirts, followed, and when she turned the corner of the house she stopped in amazement beside Gran'pa.

Back of the house the Strange Man was running in circles and dodging behind trees and bushes, now this way and now that, while right behind him came a Faun Boy with lowered head. They were so busy running they didn't notice Gran'ma and Gran'pa.

[43]

And as the old couple watched the little Faun Boy caught up with the Strange Man and butting him with all his might, sent him flying through a bunch of ferns.

Before the Strange Man could regain his feet the Faun Boy was upon him and sent him tumbling head-over-heels again.

The Strange Man scrambled to his feet when the Faun Boy tripped over some vines and without looking behind him he circled about and ran for the house.

As he reached the door, another Faun Boy rushed from the bushes and taking the Strange Man unawares, sent him flying back towards the first Faun Boy.

"Those goats will butt him to pieces!" cried Gran'ma, as she ran after the Faun Boys and tried to shoo them away.

The Faun Boys paid no attention to Gran'ma's shooing and continued to butt the Strange Man about between them until he scarcely had time to know from which side he was attacked.

When Gran'pa saw that Gran'ma's shooing had no effect upon the Faun Boys, Gran'pa ran after them and managed to catch their arms and although they struggled to get free he held them tightly.

"My gracious!" Gran'pa asked them, "Do you wish to kill that poor old man?"

"Let us go!" the Faun Boys cried, "He's a wicked magician!"

The little Faun Boy caught up with the Strange Man,
butting him with all his might.

"I thought they were goats," Gran'ma exclaimed, and she looked hard at the Faun Boys as she adjusted her glasses, "but they *are* part boys!"

The Strange Man had managed to get to his feet and without thanking Gran'pa, who still held the Faun Boys, he slipped through the bushes and disappeared.

The two Faun Boys began crying. "He was a wicked magician!" they said, "and he changed us partly into goats. We are trying to get him to change us back to our own shapes! Now you have spoiled it all!"

"Dear me!" Gran'ma cried, as she caught the two Faun Boys in her arms. "Gran'pa, you should have known better!"

"I know I should have known better now, but I didn't until they told me!" Gran'pa said. "I'm very sorry!"

Just then Janey and Johnny, who had stopped yelling to rest a little, started up again and Gran'pa and Gran'ma ran towards the house.

The door was locked.

"Open the door and we will let you out!" cried Gran'pa when he could make himself heard.

"We are tied, hands and feet," Johnny yelled, "and we can't get to the door!"

"Besides, it's locked on the outside!" Janey called.

"Let's get a fence rail and break in the door!" said Gran'pa.

But there wasn't a fence in sight.

"I'll run back to the Flying Boat and get a hatchet!" Gran'pa called, as he started away. "No doubt you will find that old Jingles, the Magician, intended changing your grandchildren into animals," the Faun Boys told Gran'ma.

"If I had him now!" Gran'ma said, stamping her foot upon the ground, "I'd tweak his long nose! That's what I'd do!"

Finally Gran'pa came running back all out of breath. "The Flying Boat and the children's Flying Machine are both gone!"

"Oh dear!" Gran'ma exclaimed, as she sat down on the ground and began crying.

The Faun Boys began butting their heads against the door, Gran'pa helping them by throwing his shoulder against it, and soon the door gave way.

Gran'ma and Gran'pa untied the children and hugged them.

The children told Gran'ma and Gran'pa of their experience. "As soon as he had learned the rhyme he was going to change us into pigs!" Janey said.

"Well, we won't let him now that we are here!" said Gran'ma, firmly.

"Oh, but you couldn't help yourself if he decided to change you into animals!" the Faun Boys told Gran'ma.

"I'd like to see him just try it!" Gran'ma said, her lips in a tight line. "I'd tweek his nose out of joint!"

"Perhaps we'd better leave the place before he returns!" Gran'pa said. "Evidently it was Jingles the Magician who took our Flying Boat!"

"Surely it must have been!" the Faun Boys said.

"Here's his large book, with the verses in, that he uses to work his magic with!" cried Johnny.

The book was too large for them to carry with them, so they hid it under some stones and scattered leaves over it so that Jingles would not be able to find it if he came back.

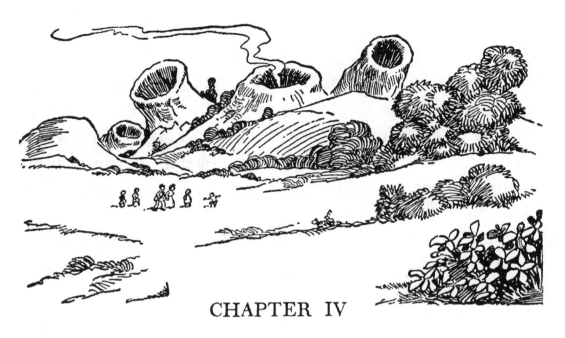

CHAPTER IV

Enter the Magic Boxing Gloves, the Wolves and the Rubber River

"THE Strange Man is called 'Jingles the Magician' because he uses rhymes to work his magic," the Faun Boys explained, as they walked from the house.

They had not gone far before they reached a large field. "This is queer!" one of the Faun Boys cried. "This field was not here when we came through a short time ago!"

About half-way across the field was a clump of bushes, and Gran'pa said, "Perhaps it would be as well to walk around it." But as they drew nearer the bushes began moving, and what seemed at first to be a flock of birds arose and flew towards them.

As the objects came closer Gran'pa saw they were Boxing Gloves; swarms of them. They flew about the little group and peppered them from all sides. Gran'pa struck them right and left with his cane, but was finally forced down. The children, Gran'ma and the Faun Boys ran as fast as they could across the field, followed by the Boxing Gloves, which swarmed about their heads like giant bees and hit against their backs and heads.

Gran'pa, still on the ground, struck right and left with his heavy cane and at each swing he brought down one or two of the Boxing Gloves.

The children, Gran'ma and the Faun Boys by this time had reached the other side of the field and dashed into the under-brush. For some reason the Boxing Gloves did not follow, but turned and flew back and began pelting Gran'pa.

Whenever Gran'pa managed to get to his feet the Boxing Gloves knocked him down, so he lay on his back and struck right and left and kicked his heels in the air to keep them from striking him.

When Johnny saw that the Boxing Gloves did not follow into the underbrush he told Gran'ma and Janey to wait where they were and breaking off a stout stick Johnny rushed back to Gran'pa's assistance.

The stick was so long and heavy that he tripped over it, but he didn't mind that—just jumped up and ran faster than ever.

Some of the Boxing Gloves met him half way and

Gran'pa struck them right and left with his cane, but was finally knocked down.

although Johnny knocked them down by the hundreds, he could not defend himself from all sides and three or four of the Boxing Gloves, striking him from behind, sent him flying to the ground.

Johnny rolled over and over, but kept his stout stick thrashing the air whenever he turned face up.

Gran'pa was still hitting the Boxing Gloves with his cane, but was getting very tired.

The ground was covered with broken Boxing Gloves, lying where Gran'pa and Johnny had struck them with their sticks.

Johnny tried to get upon his feet, but was promptly knocked down. The Faun Boys broke off large sticks and ran back into the field, where they fought the Boxing Gloves away from Gran'pa and Johnny.

The Faun Boys whipped so many of the Boxing Gloves that soon there were not enough left to injure Gran'pa and Johnny again, so as the few remaining Boxing Gloves flew at them Gran'pa and Johnny whipped these, too.

At last there were only three of the Boxing Gloves left and these were flying about one of the Faun Boys, trying to find a place to strike him.

Gran'pa ran to his assistance and as he struck at them one flew close and knocked Gran'pa's glasses from his nose, so that he could not see.

"Watch for my glasses, boys!" he cried. "Don't step on them!"

Johnny, running up, cracked one of the Boxing Gloves, but the other two kept getting behind him. Presently Johnny found himself with his back towards the Faun Boys, and a Boxing Glove coming to reach the Faun Boy did not know Johnny was there until Johnny caught it such a whack with his stick he tore it all to pieces. The Faun Boy finally knocked the thumb off the last one and the great fight with the Magic Boxing Gloves was over.

What a sight! There were thousands of torn Boxing Gloves lying about.

One of the Faun Boys found Gran'pa's glasses and handed them to him.

"That was better than fighting bumble bees when I was a boy!" Gran'pa laughed. Aside from a black and blue eye, Gran'pa was not hurt in the least.

"That surely was fun!" Johnny cried, as they reached the place where they had left Janey and Gran'ma.

"It won't be as much fun the next time!" a voice cried, and turning, they saw old Jingles the Magician sail from the Boxing Glove Bushes in the Flying Boat and disappear in the direction of his house.

"I thought he was responsible for those bushes!" said one of the Faun Boys. "You must watch out for him every minute, for all he has to do to change you into an animal is to puff his magic powder on you and say his rhyme!"

"We will watch out for him!" Gran'ma said.

The Faun Boys invited Gran'ma and Gran'pa and the children to their place to rest and have something to eat, so they led the way and without further adventure came to their tiny home.

When the Faun Boys had given Gran'pa and Gran'ma and the children food, Gran'pa said, "I don't know how we shall contrive to get the flying boat away from old Jingles."

"I should advise you not to try it," one of the Faun Boys told him, "for he will only change you into animals if he once gets you separated from each other! I should advise you to travel in the opposite direction from his place until you come to the town of Nite. Living in that town you will find an old Witch who may be able to help you reach the earth again!"

"Perhaps that will be a wise thing to do!" Gran'ma said. "For if we should get separated and one of us should be changed to an animal, the rest of us could not go home without him and we could not take him home!"

"Yes," Janey and Johnny said, "let us go to the City of Nite!"

So, thanking the Faun Boys for their hospitality, Gran'ma and Gran'pa and Janey and Johnny left them and started on their journey.

The Faun Boys had warned them to be careful of old Jingles.

"He may follow you all the way to the City of Nite and try to get each of you alone so he can say his rhymes," they said, "but once you are in the City you are safe, for we have heard that the Witch is very angry at him and will destroy him some day if she can!"

After leaving the home of the Faun Boys, Gran'ma with her arm about Janey and Gran'pa with his arm around Johnny, the travelers walked until they came to a high cliff above a river. There seemed to be no way across to the other side of the canyon except by way of a Vine Bridge.

"I can never get across that thing!" Gran'ma cried.

"We'll have to cross it or walk for miles and miles around!" Gran'pa said. For as far as they could see in either direction, the canyon was just as wide and deep as it was there.

"I just know I'd get dizzy and tumble in!" Gran'ma said.

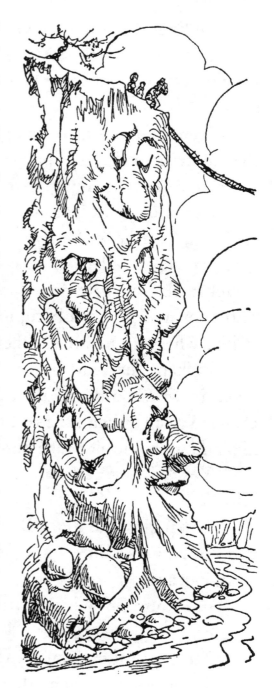

Johnny walked out upon the vine bridge and bounced it up and down.

"It is strong enough to hold us, Gran'ma!" he called back. "Put your hands over your eyes and you will be all right."

"I can't do it!" Gran'ma replied, as she sat down on the ground.

"If we only had our boat we'd fly across!" Janey said.

"Yes! If we only had our boat we'd fly home!" Gran'ma sighed.

"Maybe, after all, we had best go back to the wicked Jingles house until he goes to bed and then we may be able to get our boat!" Gran'pa suggested.

"Perhaps we had!" Johnny agreed. So they turned from the canyon and started to retrace their steps.

Suddenly Gran'pa, who was in the lead, stopped and said, "Listen! What was that?"

They all held their breaths an instant later. It was the baying of Wolves.

"They are coming in this direction!" Johnny cried.

The sound grew louder.

"Which way shall we go?" Janey asked.

"Come on everybody!" Gran'ma cried, as she lifted her skirts and ran towards the Vine Bridge.

"Wait, Gran'ma!" Janey cried. "Let Johnny help you across!" But Gran'ma kept running.

Just as she reached the edge of the canyon she stumbled and slid over the cliff.

Gran'pa, Johnny and Janey ran to the edge and looked over, expecting to see Gran'ma struggling in the river far below, but what was their surprise to see her sitting upon the top of the water, unharmed.

"Are you hurt?" Gran'pa called.

"Not a speck!" Gran'ma called back. "The river is rubber and all I did was bounce up and down!"

"Jump over and have a bounce! I wish I were up there so I could do it again! It was fine!" Gran'ma added, as she jumped up and down and bounced about like a rubber ball.

Gran'pa had almost forgotten the Wolves coming behind them, but noticing now how near they seemed, he said, "We haven't a great deal of time left, Johnny, we better jump!

The Wolves have scented us and are getting closer every minute!"

"But if we get down there, how will we ever get up again?" Johnny wondered.

"I don't know!" Gran'pa exclaimed, "but I know I shall not leave Gran'ma down there alone!" So with that, Gran'pa jumped from the cliff and turned over and over before he hit the Rubber River upon his back.

The children thought he never would stop bouncing.

By this time the children could see the Wolves in the distance.

"What shall we do?" Janey cried, wringing her hands. "If we jump down we may never get up again, if we stay here we shall be caught by the Wolves, and if we go across they will follow us!"

"We could go across and then, when the Wolves tried to follow, we could bounce the Vine Bridge and shake them off!" Johnny suggested.

"Yes, and shake them down to Gran'ma and Gran'pa! No, Johnny, that will never do!"

"Then you cross the Vine Bridge, Sis, and I'll show you what we'll do! Hurry now, before it's too late!"

Janey ran across the Vine Bridge, and when she had reached the other side Johnny drew his knife from his pocket and hacked at the vines. The small, sharp blade soon cut them in two. He was none too quick, for just as he severed

the last strand of the Vine Bridge
the Leader of the Wolves sprang toward
Johnny.

As the Vine Bridge fell Johnny jumped
and caught the loose end and went swinging across the chasm at a dizzy speed. He
managed to hold on, even if he did get quite
a bump when the Vine Bridge struck on the
other side.

When the Leader of the Wolves jumped
and missed Johnny, he flew headlong over
the cliff. Gran'pa was watching the children, but when he saw the Wolf light upon

the Rubber River he braced himself and brought his stout cane down upon the Wolf's head with such force it did not move a muscle when it had ceased bouncing.

Gran'ma, thinking the whole pack of Wolves would follow their Leader, ran to the side of the Rubber River and disappeared in a hole in the cliff.

Gran'pa followed her, and it was well he did, for as soon as Gran'ma and he started to run the Wolves jumped over the cliff to the Rubber River.

By the time the Wolves had quit bouncing Gran'pa was in the hole beside Gran'ma, and together they had rolled a large stone across the opening so the Wolves could not follow.

As for Johnny, he swung to the other side of the canyon, climbed up the Vine Bridge and finally reached the top where Janey was sitting waiting for him.

"Oh Johnny," she cried, "the Wolves jumped over the cliff after Gran'ma and Gran'pa! Look and see if you can see them anywhere."

Johnny had been so busy climbing he had known nothing of what had happened below.

Now he went to the edge and looked over. The Wolves were all at one spot on the cliff.

"Oh dear!" he cried. "They probably have caught Gran'ma and Gran'pa!"

At this Janey came to the edge and looked. She watched the pack closely for a few moments.

"No, they have not! See! The Wolves are tearing and digging at that big stone. Gran'ma and Gran'pa must be behind the stone! There must be a cave there!"

Johnny caught his sister by the shoulder and drew her hastily away from the edge of the cliff and into the bushes.

"Old Jingles in the Flying Boat!" he whispered. "I just saw a speck in the distance, coming this way!"

So the children, crouching low, ran away through the ferns and bushes.

CHAPTER V

The Beautiful Girl Tells Her Strange Story

AS SOON as Gran'pa and Gran'ma rolled the stone across the opening they walked back into the cave. It was very dark and they held their hands in front of them so they would not bump their heads if they ran into a wall. By and by Gran'pa came to some steps, and feeling his way with his cane he helped Gran'ma up the long flight. They finally reached the top and walked into a spacious cavern filled with a greenish light. They could not discover where the light came from, but they could see each other quite plainly.

Gran'pa and Gran'ma walked across the cavern until they came to a door over which hung a sign which read, "Stay out! This means you!"

"We may as well go in!" Gran'pa said, "for we cannot get out while the Wolves are at the opening!" So hand in hand they entered the door and followed a narrow passageway as it zigzagged back and forth.

Presently they came to a round room filled with a reddish light, and in the center of this room stood a large pot.

Gran'pa went up to the pot and raised the lid. As he did so the lid sprang from his hands and flew across the room. The pot began popping like a bunch of firecrackers, and white stuff flew from it up to the ceiling and rattled down about the place.

Gran'pa and Gran'ma could not find the entrance to the room again, although they went around the room four or five times.

Gran'pa discovered a hole far above their heads, and as the white stuff flew about them like hail and settled upon the floor, they kept climbing on top of it until they could reach the hole and climb through.

As they crawled into the hole something warm and sticky flowed by them, so they hurried back into the room from which they had just come. It was lucky for them that they did, for the sticky stuff poured from the hole in a stream and mixed with the white stuff which now nearly filled the room.

"It's molasses!" Gran'pa cried, as he tasted it.

"And the white stuff is popcorn!" Gran'ma cried in turn, as she took up a handful and squeezed it together into a popcorn ball.

The molasses candy continued to pour from the hole until the popcorn was covered with it. Then the room began to sway back and forth, gently at first, then faster and faster, until Gran'pa, popcorn and Gran'ma were shaken up and rolled about much the same as popcorn is in a shaker. Both Gran'pa and Gran'ma were covered with molasses and popcorn when the room ceased shaking.

"Dear me suz!" Gran'ma exclaimed. "The stuff is all in my hair!—This is a mess!"

"Yes, but just taste it, Gran'ma!" Gran'pa said. "It's fine!"

Again the room began shaking and the air grew much warmer.

"We'd better get out of this!" Gran'pa said. "There must be a fire under the room!"

So they crawled through the hole again and now the molasses candy had grown hard and did not stick to their hands.

"This must be the place the molasses came from," said Gran'ma, as they came to another room, the sides of which were covered with candy.

There seemed to be no opening at the top for the candy to come in and Gran'pa soon discovered that it came in from the bottom.

Through the hard candy at the side of the room Gran'ma thought she saw a light, and when Gran'pa pried a large piece

away with his cane they saw another long, narrow opening.

Through this they crawled until the passageway widened and they could stand up and walk.

After walking down this passageway for five or ten minutes Gran'pa and Gran'ma came to a room filled with purple light, and in the center of this room stood a large Green Jar.

"Well I won't be foolish enough to look in this one!" Gran'pa said, as he walked right past it and opened a door upon the other side. "Here we are, Gran'ma! I can see daylight, and the steps lead up to the top of the ground."

"If that is the case, I shall take a peep in this Green Jar!" Gran'ma said.

"Don't do it, Gran'ma!" Gran'pa cautioned. "Profit by our last experience!"

"Yes, but the other was a pot, and pots are always apt to boil over or do something of the sort," Gran'ma answered. "I shall look into this Green Jar and you can hold the door wide open, like this, so it won't take a moment to drop it and hurry up the steps and escape if it begins to blow popcorn or do anything of the kind."

Gran'ma took the lid from the Green Jar and thick red smoke came whirling up from it.

Gran'ma wished to run, but her knees would not let her, so she sat right down, smack! upon the floor and watched.

When the smoke thinned out Gran'ma saw the hands, then the arms, then the head of a Beautiful Girl appear above the edge of the Green Jar.

She raised her arms above her head and yawned.

When Gran'pa saw what was coming from the Green Jar he came back and helped Gran'ma to her feet.

The Beautiful Girl turned and looked at them. "Who are you?" she asked.

"Gran'ma and Gran'pa Huggins!" Gran'pa said.

"Did you open the Green Jar?" the Beautiful Girl asked.

"Gran'ma did," Gran'pa answered, "but I advised her not to!"

"Well, seeing that she opened it anyway I shall forgive you, Gran'pa!" the Beautiful Girl laughed.

"Shall we help you out?" Gran'ma asked, as she held out her hands.

"Mercy, how sticky you are!" the Beautiful Girl cried.

"We were caught in a popcorn machine!" Gran'pa laughed.

When the Beautiful Girl had been helped from the Green

Jar, Gran'pa led the way to the door and up the stairs to the ground above.

Gran'pa, Gran'ma and the Beautiful Girl came right out where Janey and Johnny were hiding. The children flew to the old people and threw their arms around their necks.

"Old Jingles sent the Wolf Pack after us," Johnny said, "for we saw him flying this way after you two had crawled into the cave!"

"Perhaps he will follow us into the cave!" said Gran'ma.

"I hope he sticks fast in the molasses candy if he does!" said Gran'pa.

"Let us fill the opening here with stones!" Johnny suggested, "so if he does follow you through the cave he will have to go all the way back for his trouble!"

So they all carried sticks and stones and filled up the mouth of the cave. When that was finished Janey asked where they had found the Beautiful Girl.

"Let us travel from here as fast as we can!" said the Beautiful Girl, "and I will tell you the story as we go along!"

As they hurried through the giant mushrooms and bushes the Beautiful Girl told them the following strange story.

"I live in the City of Nite," she began, "or at least I did live there until I was shut up in the Green Jar. I was out walking one day near the river, and as I stopped on the bank to gather some beautiful flowers growing there I came upon a Queer Horse standing in the water. At first I thought he could

"Did you open the Green Jar?" the Beautiful Girl asked.

not be alive, for he stood so still and he had no head; but as I stood gazing at him in wonderment he switched his tail and knocked some flies from his back, and I heard him say, 'There now! I hope I switched all of you off!'

"'Dear me!' I cried out aloud. 'A horse without a head talking! Whoever heard of such a thing!'

"At this the Queer Horse came out of the water and sat down upon the bank.

"'I don't see how you are able to travel about without a head!' I said.

"'Well, it is a handicap,' the Queer Horse answered, 'but I have grown used to it!'

"'Where is your head?' I asked him.

"'I ate it off!' he answered.

"'Ate it off!' I exclaimed in wonder.

"'Yes!' he replied. 'You see, I was always a sort of pig when it came to eating, and one day a Strange Man came up to me and hit me with his cane and cried, "If you don't quit your eating you'll burst! I believe if you were given all you could eat, you would eat your head off!"

"'I should like to have a trial at it!' I answered the man.

"'Then,' he said, 'You shall have it!' and he led me to a field where hay and corn and oats grew thick! 'Now,' said the Strange Man, 'Eat!'

"'So I ate and ate, until I really did eat my head off!'

"And," continued the Beautiful Girl, "I felt so sorry for

the Queer Horse I went up and patted him where his head should have been, and, lo! and behold, his head came into view!

"At this the Queer Horse was very happy, and told me he was very grateful to me. 'If I can ever be of assistance to you, I shall be very glad!' he said.

"And as we stood there talking the Strange Man came up to us and said, 'Why did you pat the Queer Horse where his head wasn't?'

"'I don't know!' I replied. 'I just felt sorry for him and wished to pat him!'

"'You've spoiled my magic!' the Strange Man said, 'and as punishment you will have to be shut up in the Green Jar!' And he struck me with his cane.

"I did not know another thing until you took the lid off the Green Jar," the Beautiful Girl told Gran'ma, as she ended her tale.

"And you don't know how long you were in the Green Jar?" asked the children.

"No, I have no recollection of any time at all. It just seems as if I had gone to sleep and just awakened."

"I never knew such things were possible," Gran'pa exclaimed, "until we came here, to the Magical Land of Noom!"

"Don't you live on the Moon?" the Beautiful Girl asked.

"No," Gran'ma answered, "we just came to the Moon. We live upon the Earth, and we shall be very glad when we can get back there, too, I tell you!"

"Why don't you return to the Earth?" the Beautiful Girl inquired.

"Old Jingles, the Magician, took our Flying Boat!" said Gran'pa. "And we are trying to escape from him now, or get our Flying Boat back, or do something, so that we can return to the Earth."

"Listen!" the Beautiful Girl cried suddenly. "What was that?"

"It sounded like thunder," Janey said. "There comes the storm cloud!"

"Let us hasten!" the Beautiful Girl cried. "Perhaps we may find shelter somewhere!"

So, catching hold of hands, they all ran as hard as they could until they came to a village.

"Here's a good place!" the girl cried, as she ran in at an open door.

They reached shelter none too soon, for the storm was upon them.

CHAPTER VI

Now We Come to the Little Old Lady and Jingle's Magic Whistle

THE wind howled, and the lightning popped and cracked, and everything grew as black as ink. The rain came down in torrents and the house in which they had taken shelter rocked and shook.

"I wonder if anyone lives here!" Gran'ma said, as she felt around the walls and turned on a light.

The room was flooded with brightness, and the Beautiful Girl saw a paper lying on a table and picked it up.

"Oh dear me!" she cried, as she sat down on a chair and buried her face in her hands.

Gran'ma ran to her and put her arms around her. "What is the matter, my dear?" she asked.

"Look at the date on this paper!" wept the Beautiful Girl. Gran'ma read, "July 24, 339,780."

"I don't understand!" said Gran'ma as the others came and stood around the Beautiful Girl.

"It was in the year 339,700 that I talked to the Queer Horse and the Strange Man put me in the jar! Oh dear! I have been in that jar for eighty years!"

"There's one consolation," said Gran'pa, gallantly, "you do not look it!"

"I know it!" the Beautiful Girl replied, "We never change much here. I did not tell you before, you see, that I am Princess Nidia of Nite, and that there has been no one to rule the City of Nite in all this time!"

"Oh, yes, there has!" Gran'ma cried. "For the Faun Boys told us there was an old Witch who ruled things in the City of Nite!"

"Then I am lost!" the Beautiful Girl cried. "For she will never let me have my throne back again!"

"We will take it away from her!" said Johnny. "It belongs to you and we will help you get it back! And we shall call you The Princess from now on!"

"I hope you can get my throne back," the Princess said, as Gran'ma wiped the tears from her eyes. "I cannot imagine who this Witch can be!"

*"It was in the year 339,700 that I talked to the Queer Horse
and the Strange Man put me in the jar!"*

"The Faun Boys told us that the Witch was an enemy of old Jingles, the wicked Magician," said Janey, "so perhaps the Witch has just been holding your throne for you until you return!"

While they had been talking the storm had increased in fury so that the windows rattled as if they would fall out.

A leak started in the roof and water dripped to the floor, where it spread on the carpet and made a black spot.

"It is one of our ink rains!" said the Princess.

Gran'ma ran to the kitchen and got a large tub which she placed where it would catch the ink and save the carpet.

"Thank you very much for doing that!" said a voice from the other side of the room. "I feel sure anyone kind enough to do and act like that would not harm a poor Little Old Lady!"

"Indeed we wouldn't harm you!" Gran'pa said. "But where are you hiding?"

"Up here!" said the Little Old Lady, as she looked out from behind a picture which covered a window.

"There is a door behind the cabinet there, and if you press the little button at the side you will see a stairway! Perhaps you would be more comfortable up here!"

"Shall we go up?" asked Gran'ma.

"Yes, let's go up and see her," the children replied.

So Johnny hunted until he found the tiny button, and the cabinet swung out from the wall, disclosing the thoroughly scoured stairway.

When they were all on the inside the cabinet swung back into place, and the little doorway was hidden.

They went up the stairs and came into a very pretty little room with soft chairs and couches standing about.

"Make yourselves comfortable," said the Little Old Lady, "while I get you a bite to eat and a cup of tea!"

From the coziness of the little room the storm could hardly be heard, and the visitors were happy, watching the Little Old Lady as she worked.

She wore a tiny little poke bonnet and a tight waist with an enormous overskirt of flowered material. Two cheery eyes full of twinkles looked out through shiny eyeglasses, and a stray white curl peeped out from beneath the back of her bonnet.

"When I heard you come running up the path, I hid," the Little Old Lady said when the tea was ready, "for no one would suspect that I had a room up here and nothing would disturb me in my retreat."

When all had eaten and Gran'ma had cleaned up the crumbs and started to wash the dishes, they were all startled by a loud thumping down stairs.

"Sh!" whispered the Little Old Lady. "Sit still while I take a peek!" She turned out the light and went to the picture and peeped through. Then she closed the picture window and turned on the light.

"Sh!" she whispered again. "Didn't I hear you talking of a wicked man? Come and see if it is he; but remember, do not make the slightest noise or he will discover us!"

When all had peeped through the picture window, and the kind old lady had closed it again the Princess said, "It is indeed the wicked Strange Man who put me in the jar!"

"It is old Jingles, the Magician!" whispered the others.

Yes, it was old Jingles, the Magician, but he was a very sorry sight. His clothes were covered with black mud and the ink rain had soaked through his hat and had run down over his face so that it was as black as coal.

He stamped his feet to shake the ink from his clothes, and wiped his face with his handkerchief; but the more he wiped it the blacker it grew.

The Little Old Lady again motioned the rest to the window and turned out the light so that they could watch old Jingles.

"Just wait until I catch them!" he muttered to himself. "I will change all of them into pigs and never let them see a mud puddle! I should have been all right if Gran'ma and Gran'pa had not come along! It's all their fault, and it was they who rescued the Princess from the Green Jar! Oh, just wait until I catch them! Then they will be sorry they ever came to the Magical Land of Noom!"

The wicked creature tried saying some of his magic rhymes to clean the ink from himself, but he did not succeed.

"I should have had all of them in my power by this time if the ink rain had not soaked my little Magic Whistle so that I cannot blow it!" And he took something from out of his pocket and wiped it with his handkerchief.

It was a Magic Whistle made of pig-skin and had little tassels hanging from it. Now the pig-skin was soaking wet and the tassels dripping ink. The more the Magician wiped the whistle, the wetter it seemed to become.

The storm had slackened by this time and old Jingles went to the window. "They cannot have gone far!" he said as he shook his fist at the black clouds disappearing in the distance, "and no matter how far they have gone, I will catch up with them when my Magic Whistle dries! And then they had better be careful!"

As the rain of ink had now ceased, the Magician went to the door and looked out. "I hope it will dry up soon," he said, "so that I can catch up with them!" And he walked out of the house.

"What had we better do?" Gran'ma asked.

"We had best stay where we are for a while," Gran'pa replied, "for evidently the ink rain has covered our tracks and he will not be able to find us, so he will go on and we can follow him."

"I must hasten to the City of Nite," cried the Princess, "and try to regain my throne. My subjects were so happy when I was there—oh, dear, I wonder how it will all turn out!"

"Perhaps the Little Old Lady can suggest something for us to do," Janey said.

The Little Old Lady thought a while and then said, "I believe it will be as well for all of you to stay here for a time. That will throw Jingles off the track. I will run over to my brothers and ask their advice. I think it would be as well for all of you to stay in this room, meanwhile, in case the Magician should return!"

Then the Little Old Lady went down a back stairway and out of the door.

"If I had known what trouble we should get into, I should never have built the Flying Machine!" said Johnny.

"Do not take all the blame, Johnny," said his sister, "for it was I who thought of most of it and then we really did not know it would fly!"

The Little Old Lady was gone for quite a while and as the others sat talking in the cozy secret room, they again heard stamping downstairs.

Gran'ma went to the picture window and peeped through. Old Jingles had returned. "I can not find their trail beyond this house!" he cried as he kicked over a chair. "If my Magic Whistle would only dry so that I could blow it and discover where they are, I could easily catch up with them and punish them!"

"Dear me!" Gran'ma whispered to the others who had gathered around the picture window to listen. "The wicked Magician seems to think we have done something very mean to him, when we are only trying to escape his clutches!"

"That is always the case," said the Princess. "Those who do the most harm always think they are the most abused when things do not go just as they wish!"

"I hope his Magic Whistle warps out of shape so that when it blows it will turn his magic right back on himself!" Johnny whispered.

The more the Magician thought of our friends escaping him the more injured he felt, and he knocked the furniture about in his anger.

At last he kicked the cabinet and loosened the little button which opened the door. "Hello!" he cried. "Here is a secret stairway!"

"Quick!" cried Gran'ma. "He has discovered the stairway! He is coming up! Run down the back way quick!"

They all ran down the back stairs as fast as they could, and of course they made a lot of noise running. The more quietly they tried to run the more they tripped and stumbled. The Magician, hearing them. knew in a moment who it was and sprang up the front stairway in pursuit. Then down the back stairs he ran too.

As Gran'pa, Gran'ma, the Princess and Janey ran down the street they saw the Little Old Lady running towards them with her three brothers.

Johnny, bracing himself at the back door, was trying to hold it so the Magician could not get out and he did succeed in holding him back until the others got a good start.

When the Magician finally forced the door open, Johnny took to his heels with the long-legged Magician close behind him. Johnny dodged this way and that until he almost caught up with the others, who, when they met the Little Old Lady and her brothers had stood still.

Just as the Magician was reaching out his hand to catch hold of John- ny's collar, Johnny remem- bered a trick he

had learned with other boys and dropped to his knees, right in front of the Magician.

The Magician rolled his eyes and started to say a rhyme, but one of the brothers clapped his hand over Jingles' mouth.

Then while two of the brothers held the Magician down, move.

The Magician rolled his eyes and started to say a rhyme, but one of the brothers clapped his hand over Jingles' mouth.

Then while two of the brothers held the Magician down, the other ran to the house and came back with ropes. Soon the Magician was tied so that he could not move a muscle and a handkerchief was tied across his mouth.

By this time many people had gathered about and it was suggested that old Jingles be given a seat in the ducking pool.

"Now," said the Little Old Lady, "you folks had better be on your way! We will keep the Magician here as long as possible."

So Gran'pa, Gran'ma, Johnny, Janey and the Princess stayed only long enough to see the Magician soused up and down in the water two or three times and then they hastened out of town.

The brothers ducked the wicked Magician up and down in the pond until they grew tired, then others took their places and they kept this up for two hours. Then the Magician was placed in the stocks and his hands and feet firmly padlocked so that he could not get away.

CHAPTER VII

THE SOFT-VOICED COW MEETS THE WITCH AND THE INVISIBLE PEOPLE

AFTER leaving the village in which the Magician was a prisoner, Gran'ma, Gran'pa, the Princess and the children ran until they were tired, and coming to a quiet shady place they sat down to rest.

"I do not believe I have run so hard since I was a girl," said Gran'ma as she fanned herself.

Just then they heard a noise in the bushes and all sprang to their feet, but sat down again with sighs of relief when a Cow walked up to them.

The Cow wore a pretty bonnet and a velour waist; her skirt was of velvet with flowers embroidered around the edge.

As she came up to the little group she shook the wrinkles out of her apron and sat down facing them.

"How do you do, everybody!" the Cow said in a soft voice, as she smiled at all.

Everybody greeted the Soft-Voiced Cow in a kindly manner.

"I saw you running across the field," said the Soft-Voiced Cow, "and you looked as if you were running away from something."

"We were," Gran'ma said. "We were running away from Old Jingles the Magician, who wants to change us into animals."

"Dear me suz!" exclaimed the Soft-Voiced Cow. "Is he that wicked?"

"Yes indeed he is," Janey said, and she told of their experiences, and of that of the Princess.

"If he follows you, he may find me when he comes this way," said the Soft-Voiced Cow. "So if you do not mind my company, I will go with you to the City of Nite. I should not care to meet so wicked a Magician."

"We should be greatly pleased to have your company," they told the Soft-Voiced Cow.

When they had rested, Gran'pa said they better begin travel on; so the Soft-Voiced Cow took Gran'ma and the Princess and Janey on her back and the little party started on their way.

The Old Woman caught the Soft-Voiced Cow's tail and began dragging her back.

They passed through dense groves of giant mushrooms and at times these were so thick they had to bend them to one side in order to pass.

When they grew hungry the children told Gran'ma and Gran'pa that the mushrooms were cake, so they ate of these.

After leaving the forest of mushrooms the path led through very rocky country and as they turned a cliff the party came upon a spring bubbling from the rocks and splashing down into a small stream far below.

There were a number of cups near the spring, so the children ran up and took a drink. "Oh hurry!" they cried, "It's a soda water spring!"

After drinking all they wished they again set out upon their journey. When they finally left the rocky country and came upon a level stretch of road they saw approaching them an Old Woman.

Gran'ma, the Princess and Janey had dismounted from the back of the Soft-Voiced Cow, for they did not wish to tire her.

When the Old Woman came up to them, she caught the Soft-Voiced Cow by the tail and began dragging her back the way the party had come.

Gran'pa was for making her let go of the Soft-Voiced Cow's tail, but the Soft-Voiced Cow spoke gently and said, "Let her be; she is evidently an ill mannered person or she would not treat a stranger in this manner!"

However, the Old Woman dragged the Soft-Voiced Cow down the road so fast the friction of the cow's feet upon the roadway made them burn.

So the Soft-Voiced Cow turned to the Old Woman and said, "I wish you would please let go of my tail! I do not care to travel in the direction you are taking me and besides you are making my feet burn."

But the Old Woman kept right on and paid no attention to the cow.

When the Soft-Voiced Cow had been dragged back upon the road for about a mile with the little party following her, the Soft-Voiced Cow turned her head to the Old Woman and said in her gentle way, "My dear lady, I must insist that you let go of my tail, for you are delaying our party! We wish to go in the opposite direction! And if you drag me three more steps, I shall have to raise my heels and upset you!"

At this, Gran'pa caught the Old Woman's arm and said, "Why do you drag the Soft-Voiced Cow in this manner?" The Old Woman stopped and gazed at Gran'pa for a moment, "Does this Cow belong to you?" she asked.

"Of course not!" Gran'pa replied.

"Does she belong to anyone in your party?" the Old Woman asked.

"Of course not!" Gran'pa replied.

"Then," said the Old Woman, "in that case, the Cow does not belong to you nor anyone else that you know of, so she must be lost. And anything which is lost belongs to the one who finds it! Therefore, since I found the Cow she belongs to me, so I will take her home and make ox tail soup out of her!"

"Did you ever hear the like?" cried the Princess. "Do not let her take the Soft-Voiced Cow to make soup of!"

The Old Woman again began dragging the Soft-Voiced Cow down the road.

"Stand aside!" said the Soft-Voiced Cow. "ONE, TWO, THREE! There!" She raised her heels in the air and upset the Old Woman. "I promised that I would do it if you dragged me three more steps "

The Old Woman scrambled to her feet and shook her fist at Gran'ma. "You will pay for this!" she cried. "Just wait!"

And as the travelers and the Soft-Voiced Cow resumed their journey, the Old Woman followed right behind them muttering in an undertone, "You will pay for this!"

When they had gone but a little way beyond the place where they had met the Old Woman, Johnny who was ahead of the others found ten cans. With these he came running back.

"Here are ten cans of ox tail soup!" he said, as he offered them to the Old Woman.

"I don't want them!" the Old Woman cried. "I want the Soft-Voiced Cow and I will have her if I have to follow you all around the Moon!"

"You are a most unreasonable Old Woman!" said the Princess. "You don't try to be happy! When you get what you want it seems to make you discontented!"

The Old Woman did not answer, but ran around the party and down the road ahead of them. "You just wait!" she cried again. "You will all be sorry!"

"Let's not pay any attention to her any more!" said the Soft-Voiced Cow. "She is very disagreeable and has delayed us long enough as it is!"

The Old Woman could run very fast and she soon disappeared around the bend in the road. They heard her clapping and shouting. When the travelers reached the bend in the road a strange sight met their eyes.

As far as they could see before them and to either side was a great bog.

Gran'pa went up to it and pushed his cane into the edge. It was very soft.

"We shall have to walk around it," Gran'pa said, "for we should sink out of sight if we attempted to cross it!"

When Gran'pa wiped his cane off in the grass, he felt that it was very sticky, and touching his finger to the bog he tasted it. "Molasses candy mud!" he cried.

"This is very unfortunate!" said the Princess as she looked about. "We shall lose a lot of time walking around the molasses candy bog!"

"I told you that you would be sorry!" cried a voice behind them, and looking around they saw the Old Woman standing on a little hill shaking her fist at them. "I made it with my magic!" she called, "and you will never get across it!"

"The unreasonable wicked creature!" Gran'ma cried as she started after the Old Woman. "I will tweek your nose for you if I catch you!"

The Old Woman did not tarry long, but struck out over the hill with Gran'ma close behind her. Gran'ma ran after the Old Woman and the others followed. The Old Woman made for a little house not far away and as she jumped through the door, she, the house and all disappeared.

"Well!" Gran'pa cried as he came up to Gran'ma. "We are rid of her at any rate!"

"I hope we shall never see her again," said the Soft-Voiced Cow. "Like most disagreeable people she isn't satisfied unless everyone else is uncomfortable, depressed and so unhappy."

"We may as well start walking around the molasses

[87]

candy bog," said the Princess, "for we are losing so much time old Jingles may catch up with us!"

"I have a suggestion," said the Soft-Voiced Cow, "which may be helpful. Let us all walk down to the molasses candy bog, and when we are at the edge I will take you all on my back and carry you some distance along the bank, so that you will not leave any footprints. Then when the Magician comes along he will not be able to track you!"

"That is an excellent idea!" said Gran'pa. "Let us act upon the Soft-Voiced Cow's suggestion!" So they all walked down to the molasses candy bog.

The Soft-Voiced Cow took Gran'ma, Janey and the Princess upon her back and carried them far down the bank; then she returned and carried Gran'pa and Johnny to where the others were waiting.

But as they walked the bank gradually curved in until in a short time they were walking in the direction from which they had just come.

"This will never do," said Gran'pa coming to a stop, "for we are returning from whence we came."

And when they walked back along the bank the same thing happened. Everything went swinging before them in long, sweeping circles. They couldn't make heads or tails of the shore line.

"Let us try walking away from the molasses candy bog," said Johnny, "and see what happens then!"

So they turned their backs to the bog and started walking away from it. Sure enough, when they did this the bog began to fade away, and soon it disappeared entirely!

"Whee!" cried the children. "We can go ahead!"

The travelers had lost a lot of valuable time, so they hastened across the fields where the bog had been.

"You see!" said the Princess, "Johnny was right! The Old Woman's magic was as contrary as herself, for when the molasses candy bog thought we did not care whether we crossed it or not, it disappeared."

As the travelers walked along, they saw numbers of small animals running about.

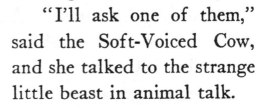

"I wonder where these little animals were when the great molasses bog was here!" Janey said looking at them curiously.

"I'll ask one of them," said the Soft-Voiced Cow, and she talked to the strange little beast in animal talk.

When the little animal answered, the Soft Voiced Cow rolled over on the ground with laughter and when at last she could speak she said, "I asked the animal where it was when the bog was here, and it said there never had been a bog here. Said it had lived here for years and the ground had always been as it is now, except after a hard rain, so you see the Old Woman only made us believe we saw a bog here, when in reality there was none at all."

"It's queer," exclaimed Gran'pa, "but I certainly tasted molasses candy on my cane! In fact," he said, looking at the cane, "there is still some on it now!"

"Let me taste it!" Gran'ma cried. "Yes," she said, "it is molasses candy!"

"Well at any rate we are not troubled with the bog now!" Janey mused.

Across the fields rose high mountains.

"I wonder if we shall be able to find a path through the mountains!" Gran'pa said.

"I think those are the mountains bordering the City of Nite!" said the Princess. "And if that is the case we have not very much farther to travel."

But the mountains were farther away than the travelers thought, for after walking for an hour they came to a rise in the ground from which they looked across miles and miles of beautiful valley country. Gran'ma and Gran'pa said it was almost as pretty as the country round the farm back home.

Down in the valley a little way they saw a tiny house and walked in that direction. When they came to the front gate and called no one answered, so they walked in and knocked at the door.

As no one answered the knock they walked around to the back door and looked inside the kitchen, for the door was open. There on the stove were pots and pans filled with food which was cooking; and as they watched, one of the pots raised itself from the stove and poured its contents into another pot. Then another pot moved across the stove and its lid came off and hung itself in the air, while a large spoon raised itself from the back of the stove and stirred the contents of the pot.

"Shall we go in?" Janey whispered, as they all hesitated on the step.

Gran'pa raised his cane and knocked three times on the door sill.

"What was that?" cried a man's voice from the front part of the house.

"Something hammered upon the door!" a woman's voice in the kitchen answered. "But I can see nothing outside to cause the noise!"

Gran'pa raised his cane and gave three more knocks.

"Did you ever!" the woman's voice cried. "I was looking right at the spot where the noise came from and I could not see a thing!"

Evidently the man had come to the kitchen door and stood near the woman, for the travelers heard him speak right at the back door.

"What could it have been, Ella?" he said.

Gran'pa turned and winked at the others and again rapped three times with his cane upon the door sill.

"There! You hear for yourself, Jules! There must be an invisible person knocking at the door!"

"Is anyone there?" asked the man's voice.

"We are standing right here in plain sight!" Gran'ma replied.

"Dear me!" the woman's voice said. "I can see no one, can you, Jules?"

"I can't see anyone!" Jules answered. "Whoever it is must be invisible!"

"It's the Princess of Nite, Janey and Johnny, Gran'ma and Gran'pa Huggins!" Gran'pa said. "We can see ourselves easily, but you are invisible to us!"

"Had we better ask them in?" Ella inquired of the man.

"Yes, do come in!" he said in answer, and as Gran'pa

was nearest the door, he walked in first and bumped right into the Invisible Man.

"Please excuse me!" Gran'pa said. "I am sorry, but I did not see you!"

"That's all right," the Invisible Man replied in a cheery voice. "I was standing right in the doorway and I should have moved out of your way!"

His voice now came from the other side of the kitchen. "We will stand over at this side of the room until all of you have gone into the dining room. We were about to have dinner, and if you will take pot luck we shall be pleased to have you dine with us."

"That is nice of you!" Gran'ma said as she and the others walked into the dining room and sat down at the table.

"It is strange to hear people speak and not be able to see them!" said Janey.

Johnny felt something brush against his leg and when he felt down there he touched fur. "Here's a kitten!" he cried, as he picked it up and held it upon his lap. All could hear the kitten purring as Johnny stroked it's back, but it was invisible too.

There were only two plates upon the table when the visitors entered the dining room, but now five more plates seemed to place themselves.

"Everybody pull up chairs!" said the Invisible Man, as he caught hold of Gran'ma's chair and tried to pull it towards the table. "Please excuse me," he laughed when he felt the weight and knew that one of his guests was in it.

All pulled their chairs up to the table, Ella suggesting that the visitors be seated first so that she and Jules would know just where they were.

So all of the party presently were seated at the table and Ella brought in the food from the kitchen.

It was strange for Gran'pa, Gran'ma, the children and the Princess to see the dishes of food come floating in from the kitchen, and it seemed as strange for Jules and Ella to hear the voices of invisible guests and see their knives and forks rise from the table to cut their food.

When Jules had passed everything and all had helped themselves he asked where they were traveling and where they had come from.

"It's a long story," Gran'pa said.

Then Gran'ma told him of how they had come to the Moon, and why they were traveling to the City of Nite.

"But the wicked Magician will not be able to see you," said Jules, "for you are invisible!"

"No," Gran'ma answered, "we are visible to him, but the chances are that he will not be able to see you!"

"If that is the case, and he should pass here we will do our best to help you!" said Ella.

When the visitors had finished their dinner they thanked Jules and Ella and asked if they might be excused.

[95]

"We are anxious to get to the City of Nite so that we can assist the Princess in regaining her throne, and try to get our Flying Boat so that we can return to the Earth," they explained.

The Invisible Man and Woman said they understood the visitors' hurry, and told them to stop in to see them if they passed that way again.

Just then the Soft-Voiced Cow put her head in at the door and asked if they were ready to start.

When the Invisible Man and Woman heard the Soft-Voiced Cow speak they asked if they had forgotten to invite some of the party in to dinner.

"It's the Soft-Voiced Cow," explained the Princess. "She has been eating her dinner of grass out in the back yard!"

"I can scarcely believe there is a Cow there!" said the voice of Ella. "Would the Cow mind if I touched her to see if I can feel her?"

The Soft-Voiced Cow laughed heartily at this and stood still while Ella patted her.

After a lot of reaching around in the air, Gran'pa and the rest succeeded in shaking hands with their invisible friends.

"Funny how pleasant people keep out of sight," Gran'ma said as her party started down the walk.

"Thank you so much!" they all cried. "We hope to see you again some time!"

At this the Invisible Man and Woman laughed and replied, "And we hope to see you again some time, too!"

CHAPTER VIII

Tiptoe, the Dancing Master, Uses His Magic Umbrella

AFTER traveling for a long time the travelers finally came to the mountains and as they walked up a path amongst the rocks they heard someone talking.

It proved to be a queer little man, no larger than Johnny.

He was seated near a large stone in the shade of a small umbrella, and he was talking to himself.

When he heard the footsteps of the party, he arose to his feet and made a low bow, sweeping the dust from the ground with the top of his high hat.

"Good afternoon!" he called cheerily.

Then seeing the Princess, who had been walking behind Gran'pa, he rushed towards her and threw himself at her feet.

"It's my old Dancing Master, Tiptoe!" cried the Princess as she pulled the little man to his feet and gave him a hug before introducing him to Gran'pa and the others.

"What are you doing way out here in the mountains?" the Princess asked when they had all taken seats around the Dancing Master.

The Dancing Master took out a red handkerchief and wiped his nose-glasses carefully. "It's really a long story," he replied. "Won't you tell me where you have been for eighty years first?" he inquired of the Princess.

The Princess told him of her strange adventure with the Queer Horse and all that had happened up to the time she was rescued from the Green Jar by Gran'ma.

When she had finished her story the Dancing Master took Gran'ma's hand and kissed it.

"Everyone in the City of Nite owes you a debt of gratitude, Gran'ma," he said, "and in some manner or other I, for one, hope to repay you!"

"Oh it wasn't anything!" Gran'ma cried. "I just saw the Green Jar and opened it because I was inquisitive. Of course we are very glad that we rescued the Princess from the Green Jar but we do not deserve any credit for it!"

Janey, who was anxious to hear the Dancing Master's story, again asked Tiptoe how he happened to be in the mountains.

"The day you disappeared," the Dancing Master said, turning to the Princess, "I was to have given you a lesson, don't you remember? And I was on my way to the Castle when I saw people running in all directions about the City of Nite. I inquired of one why they were so excited. 'Don't you know?' he answered. 'The Beautiful Princess has disappeared! Completely vanished!'"

"When I heard this I ran with all speed to the Castle. I had the right to enter at any time in the day," he explained to the children, "so I ran right up to the ball-room, for I heard voices in loud discord coming from there!"

"There I found a strange looking woman, with long straggly hair and a long nose, shaking her walking stick at the Princess' Ladies in Waiting.

"What is going on here?" I cried as I ran up to the group of ladies.

"'This strange creature claims to be the Princess and says that a Magician has transformed her into an old woman,' the Ladies in Waiting answered. 'We do not believe she is telling us the truth!'

"I could not believe it myself," added the Dancing Master, "but still I have heard of stranger things, so I said to the Ladies in Waiting, 'Perhaps she really is the Princess!'

"At first I could not get any of the ladies to agree with me," the Little Man went on, "and really, to tell the truth, I could not blame them much for as the days went by the queer creature who said she had been changed from our own Beautiful Princess into this ugly woman did such disagreeable things to the Ladies in Waiting they all moved from the Castle, and would not have anything to do with her. After a while I discovered that the old woman was not the Princess.

"You must know that by this time no one ever went near the old woman, who lived alone and kept herself shut up in a room away in the top of the Castle tower. One night, as I was passing the Castle, I heard a window creak far above my head, and looking up I saw the old woman, seated in an umbrella, fly out of the tower window and go speeding away out of sight. Then I knew that she was a witch!

"I ran home as fast as I could and told Mrs. Tiptoe what I had seen.

"We were so excited at first we couldn't think of a thing to say. We just looked at each other.

"Mrs. Tiptoe was one of the Ladies in Waiting to the Princess!" the Dancing Master explained to Gran'ma. "Finally my good wife cried, 'I knew it all along! It is not our beautiful Princess. Who knows but that this wicked Witch has taken the Princess and hidden her away somewhere!'

"'I will go see this Witch and talk to her myself!' Mrs. Tiptoe cried, an instant later and I could not dissuade her. Although she might have known it would lead to trouble, she put on her bonnet and ran to the Castle!

"Of course I followed. We went up the palace steps together and right in at the door. The Palace was a sight!" exclaimed the Little Man. "No one ever went there and there were papers and cobwebs all over the place. No one cleaned any of the rooms, for no one would have anything to do with that disagreeable old creature! So we went through the Palace until we came to the rooms the old hag used for her living quarters, and there we found proof that it indeed was not our beloved Princess!"

Here the poor Dancing Master fell to weeping so violently the Princess came and placed her arm over his shoulder, and Gran'pa and Gran'ma looked far across the valley, their eyes swimming in tears.

When the Dancing Master had dried his eyes he continued, "We found many charms and implements of magic. Rabbit's feet, and other things of the kind. Then, too, in corners and upon shelves about the room were jars of peculiar powder with labels which we could not read pasted upon them. In the center of the room was an iron kettle and queer designs had been traced about on the marble floor with black, green and yellow paint.

"'I knew she was a witch!" my wife cried. 'Go call the Guards while I wait here to see that she does not escape!'

"I ran out of the castle in hopes that I might bring the Guards and place them in the room before the old witch returned. But try as hard as I could, I could not find a Guard anywhere; they had all gone to parties or were off on their vacations, so I ran back to the castle. 'We will capture the Witch ourselves!' I cried as I ran into the Witch's room."

"I expected to see Mrs. Tiptoe sitting there with a stern expression on her face, just waiting for the Witch's return, but what was my surprise and consternation to see the Witch herself leering at me with her wicked smile.

"The Witch told me I was the only one who knew for sure she was not the Princess, so she would send me in search of Mrs. Tiptoe. 'For,' said the wicked creature, 'by the time you find your wife, you will have learned better than to tell anyone that I am not the Princess!'"

"And," continued the Dancing Master, "without saying another word she opened her Magic Umbrella and pointed her crooked cane at me. I was forced to step into the Magic Umbrella. As I did so it shot out of the window so fast I could scarcely catch my breath. Over the town of Nite I flew and over the mountains I soared, until finally the Magic Umbrella lit upon the ground miles and miles away from everybody. It was days and days before I met anyone to talk to—awfully lonely life, but since then I have heard from people in different towns that the wicked creature still rules the City of Nite!" the Dancing Master finished, "but I have never ventured back there since she made me fly from the place."

"And how long is it since you left the City of Nite?" Gran'ma inquired.

"I was forced to step into the Magic Umbrella."

The Dancing Master looked at the handle of his umbrella. "I have put a notch on the handle for each year," he replied, and when he had counted them he said "Seventy-six years!"

"And you have never been able to find your wife?" asked Gran'pa.

The Dancing Master shook his head sadly.

"If we ever get to the City of Nite I will tweek the nose of that wicked Witch!" cried Gran'ma, as she snapped her fingers in the air.

"And if I have a good chance," said the Soft-Voiced Cow, who had wandered up and had listened to the Dancing Master's story, "I will raise my heels and upset her!"

"I do not know what to suggest," said the Dancing Master. "Perhaps it would be best if we do not return to the City of Nite, for the wicked creature may work harm to us all!"

"*I* shall return to the City of Nite," said the Princess, as she stamped her foot, "for it is my throne and I will have it back!"

"And I will go with you," Gran'pa cried, "and help you regain your throne!"

"We'll all go!" Gran'ma cried, jumping to her feet and smoothing out her apron.

"It is a long hard road!" said the Dancing Master doubtfully. "Why not live here in the mountains where we shall not be troubled, for I myself have lived here for the last ten years and it is very agreeable!"

They followed the Dancing Master as he led the way up over the rocks until they came to a level place, at the back of which was a Cave.

The Dancing Master, with timber which he had hewn from the trees, had made the front part of a tiny Cottage, with a wide piazza to fit the opening of the Cave.

"This has been my home for ten years!" he said, "and the absence of Mrs. Tiptoe from it is all that keeps my happiness from being complete!"

When all had entered the little Cottage Cave, the Dancing Master set the table and with Gran'ma's help made tea.

When all were seated about the room (with the exception of the Soft-Voiced Cow, who was too large to enter the tiny doorway) the Princess said to Mr. Tiptoe, "Tell me of my father and mother. What did they think when they heard that I had changed into a wicked looking Witch?"

"Your dear mother, the Queen, came to the City of Nite at once," the Dancing Master answered, "but the Witch who pretended to be you would not see her, saying that it would not do to see her mother as she was too ugly; so your mother returned without seeing the wicked creature at all!"

"I am sure your Mamma would have known it was not you!" said Janey.

During all this time Johnny had been very thoughtful. Presently he asked, "When you traveled in the Magic Umbrella, how did you guide it?"

"The first time I rode in it," the Dancing Master answered, "I did not guide it. I came down without any thought of where I was going, but as there was not a thing near by, I stepped back into the Magic Umbrella and wished it would fly to a town, and sure enough it flew there! All you have to do," he continued, "is to sit in it and wish it to go somewhere!"

"Then," said Johnny, "I have a suggestion! Let us all sit in the umbrella and wish it to take us to the City of Nite!"

"That's a fine idea!" cried the Princess, clapping her hands. "Let us go there immediately!"

The Dancing Master carried the Magic Umbrella out upon the level place in front of the Cottage-Cave. Then he stood and scratched his head.

"Can we all get into it?" he wondered.

It was scarcely large enough for them all, even if they sat upon the edges, and while they were all squeezing into the Magic Umbrella the Soft-Voiced Cow walked up.

"What about the Soft-Voiced Cow!" cried Janey.

"I shall not leave her behind if we never get to the City of Nite, and if we never get back our Flying Boat!" cried Gran'ma, as she scrambled out of the Magic Umbrella.

"Nor I either!" Gran'pa exclaimed as he too hopped from the Magic Umbrella.

Johnny and Janey followed them, and they all went over to the Soft-Voiced Cow and sat down on the grass.

"You may spoil everything!" said the Soft-Voiced Cow. "Please do not think of me! Get into the umbrella and go with the Princess to the City of Nite and I will follow as best I can!"

"Shan't do it!" said Gran'ma firmly.

"Wouldn't think of it!" cried Gran'pa.

"I have it!" cried the Dancing Master. "I hate to leave the Soft-Voiced Cow here, so if the Princess will excuse me, I will journey afoot with you and she can wish herself in the City of Nite!"

"I believe it would be best for the Princess to wish herself with her Mamma!" said Janey. "Then her Mamma and Daddy can advise her what to do!"

"Your advice is good," said the Princess, and kissing them all goodbye, she stepped into the Magic Umbrella and flew up over the mountains leaving the little group of friends watching her with tear-dimmed eyes. She was such a good, dear, sweet, beautiful Princess that they hated to see her go.

"I have a few things to pack," said the Dancing Master, "but I shall soon catch up with you. Keep to the right on all paths up over the mountain and I shall soon be along!"

Johnny took the lead, then came Gran'ma, Janey and Gran'pa. Up, up they toiled; up so high they could look back and see the valley stretched far below them like a picture map.

At one place they came to a waterfall which dashed straight out of the solid rock and fell for hundreds of feet in a roar of snow-white water.

The trees about the side of the river had soft green foliage, different from any trees they had ever seen before.

Presently, as they had traveled far and the climb had been very steep, they decided it would be well to rest and wait for the Dancing Master to catch up with them.

"I'm getting hungry!" Gran'ma said, "I didn't eat much at the Dancing Master's house!"

"I wish I had a mince pie in my pocket!" said Gran'pa, winking slyly at Janey.

Johnny walked over to where the river ran smoothly before it again plunged down the mountain side.

"Come here!" he cried excitedly. "Look at the strange fish!"

Gran'pa, Janey and Gran'ma came running to the edge of the stream, but the Soft-Voiced Cow continued eating the velvety grass where she had first stopped. It was the most delicious grass she had tasted in a long, long time.

"Perhaps we can catch some," said Gran'ma, "and fry them for our supper!"

Johnny felt through his pockets. "I had a fishing line in one of my pockets!" he said.

"You used the line on the Flying Machine!" said Janey. "Oh, isn't that too bad!"

"Here's the hook!" said Johnny, as he turned his pocket wrong side out and showed them the hook fastened in the cloth.

Gran'pa took his pocket knife and cut the hook out of Johnny's pocket.

"I have some string," Gran'pa said. "I know it always comes in handy, so I put a lot in my pocket before Gran'ma and I started up here!"

Gran'pa cut a pole and fixed the line while Johnny found a few worms under a stone.

At the first cast of the line into the water Gran'pa pulled out a lovely fish. It had a blue head. The body was white, with a round yellow spot on each side.

Gran'pa caught three more like the first and then six brown fish, round and flat with one side of them a golden yellow.

While Johnny and Gran'pa were building the fire and cutting sticks to broil the fish on, Janey found some worms and caught five queer fish with holes right through them.

"Aren't they queer?" she cried as she put her fingers through the holes and carried them over to Johnny.

Gran'ma caught four very fat fish which looked more like balls than fish.

"I don't believe these are good to eat," she said as she

brought them over to the fire. "They feel so light and empty and puffy!"

Gran'pa and Johnny had by this time fixed the first fish upon the sticks and they were beginning to broil.

Gran'ma sniffed the air. "Smells like they might be good, but they don't smell like fish!" she said.

When the fish were done, Gran'pa and Johnny turned them over on a clean white stone. "Eggs!" Johnny shouted.

Indeed the first fish were nothing more nor less than ordinary eggs.

The other brown fish, one side of which was golden yellow, turned out to be brown bread and butter when it was broiled.

Janey's fish turned out to be doughnuts, and Gran'ma's changed to cream puffs when placed before the fire.

"This is fit for a king!" Gran'ma cried as she sampled the egg fish.

"I wonder why Mr. Tiptoe doesn't come," Gran'pa said. "He must have packed up quite a load! Guess I'll run down the mountain and help him along!"

"Indeed you won't!" cried Gran'ma as she caught his coat tails.

"You don't know when old Jingles the Magician may catch up with us! I think now that we have finished our dinners, it would be best if we hurried on!"

"Yes, let's go on!" Johnny suggested. "Mr. Tiptoe knows the way and will soon catch up with us!"

CHAPTER IX

Johnny and Janey Grow Very Tall and Have Some Strange Adventures

THE path led up over a ledge in the mountain, revealing a pretty little valley between the high cliffs on either side. The grass under their feet was soft as velvet as they walked toward a tiny white bridge over a brook.

"This ought to be good ground for growing potatoes!" said Gran'pa, stopping to gaze about him at the charming valley.

Gran'ma was ahead and had started across the little bridge when the rest saw her trip and almost fall. She managed to save herself by catching the railing, and the others, as they ran toward her, heard a bell tinkling up one side of the cliff.

"Some mean person stretched a wire across the bridge and I tripped over it!" Gran'ma cried, as she showed the others the offending wire.

Johnny caught hold of it to pull it loose, but gave a whoop and started jumping up and down.

The bell up the cliff tinkled each time Johnny jumped.

Janey, wishing to help her brother, caught Johnny's hands to pull them from the tiny wire, and with a cry she too began hopping up and down and shouting for help.

As Gran'ma reached for Janey, Gran'pa pushed her aside. "Don't touch them!" he yelled. "It's an electric wire! Stand back!" And with this Gran'pa took the crooked handle of his cane and jerked the wire from Johnny's hands.

Johnny and Janey sat down with a bump upon the tiny bridge.

"O—oh Brud," Janey laughed. "Wasn't that funny!"

"It's funny now," answered her brother, "but it wasn't pleasant when I first touched the wire! It felt as if I was being stretched out about six feet tall!"

"You *are* getting longer!" Gran'ma cried, as she helped Johnny to his feet.

"Look at Janey!" he laughed. "Her dress is getting too short for her! Ha! Ha!"

"I don't see anything funny about it!" Gran'pa said reprovingly. "In fact, it may be very serious!"

Johnny sobered up and twisted about to see himself. Both Johnny and Janey had grown two feet taller and were still growing.

Their clothes were far too short to cover them and they looked ridiculous. Janey began crying as the Soft Voiced Cow caught up with them.

"Whatever in the world has happened?" she asked as she sat down upon the wire.

Gran'pa cried "LOOK OUT!" but he was too late. The Soft-Voiced Cow jumped three feet in the air and started across the valley, kicking her heels and mooing, while the tiny wire wrapped itself about her tail.

With Gran'pa in the lead, waving his cane, they all ran after the Soft Voiced Cow.

"Wait a minute!" Gran'pa shouted. "I'll pull it off with my cane! WAIT A MINUTE!"

But the Soft-Voiced Cow continued running until the wire became tangled in a bush and was pulled from her tail.

When she was free the Soft-Voiced Cow rolled head over heels and turned a complete somersault before she sat up and looked around wonderingly.

"I do believe I lost my cud!" she exclaimed as Gran'pa and the children came up to her.

"Your cud!" Janey exclaimed in wonderment.

"Yes, my chewing-gum!" replied the Soft-Voiced Cow. "All cows have cuds for chewing gum."

"Perhaps you left it at the Little Man's house!" Janey suggested.

"No! The Soft-Voiced Cow wasn't in the house!" Gran'ma said, as she joined the group.

"Look in all your pockets!" Johnny suggested.

"Maybe you swallowed it," Gran'pa remarked.

"Oh, maybe I did!" the Soft-Voiced Cow replied. "Sometimes I do when I'm excited! Yes, here it is!" and with a contented sigh the Soft-Voiced Cow began chewing.

Johnny and Janey had stopped growing by this time and it was well they had, for their clothes were now so tight they were very uncomfortable.

"Now, everyone keep away from the wire!" Gran'pa advised, pointing to it with his stick. "Let us get away from here as fast as we can and watch our steps from now on!"

"It's funny the Soft-Voiced Cow doesn't grow taller!" Johnny said to Janey as they followed the others across the valley. "She hasn't grown a bit!"

"I am glad she hasn't," Janey replied, "for it certainly is uncomfortable to be so tall!"

Janey was a head taller than Gran'ma, and Johnny was still taller than she was. Their stockings came nowhere near their knees.

"I thought I heard a bell tinkling when we touched the wire!" Gran'ma said as they walked along.

"So did I," the Soft-Voiced Cow laughed. "When I did not have the wire fastened about my tail!"

As the travelers came around the bend of the mountain and left the little valley, they saw before them a little hut such as one sees at fair-grounds and pleasure resorts.

The Soft-Voiced Cow jumped three feet in the air and started across the valley, kicking her heels and mooing.

A queer little man wearing a stove pipe hat leaned over the counter at the front of the hut and smiled at them. "Was it you who rang the bell?" he inquired.

"I guess all of us rang it!" Gran'ma replied, for she saw the little man was going to be agreeable.

The little man turned and looked at the dial at the side of the hut; the indicator pointed to four.

"You rang the bell four times," he said in a matter of fact voice, "so you get four cigars!" and he handed out four large black cigars.

"I don't smoke!" said the Soft-Voiced Cow, with a laugh.

"Nor I either!" Gran'ma, Janey and Johnny chimed in together.

"Then this gentleman may have them!" said the man as he handed the four fat cigars to Gran'pa. "Someone has to have them, you know," he said, "for each time the bell rings I have to give someone a cigar!"

Gran'pa put the cigars in his pocket. "I'll smoke them after a while!" he said.

"But they'll melt!" cried the man. "You must eat them right away!"

Gran'pa pulled the cigars from his pocket, then with a smile he handed one to each of the children and to Gran'ma.

The cigars were made of chocolate candy. "Won't you have one?" Gran'pa asked, offering the remaining cigar to the Soft-Voiced Cow.

"No, thanks," the Soft-Voiced Cow replied, "I hardly ever eat candy!"

"I have some nice buttered pop-corn!" the man suggested.

"I might have a basket of pop-corn, if you have it to spare!" the Soft-Voiced Cow laughed.

"You shall have it!" the man replied, as he reached behind the counter and lifted a basket of pop-corn to the Soft-Voiced Cow.

The Soft-Voiced Cow took one mouthful of the pop-corn and then blew it out of her mouth.

Gran'ma looked at her in surprise.

"It has mustard on it!" the Soft-Voiced Cow said, as the tears streamed out of her eyes and she sneezed two or three times.

"Mustard!" the man at the counter exclaimed, looking at the cow with a queer expression. "Of course it has mustard on it! I put it on to keep the pop-corn hot!"

Gran'pa winked at Johnny.

"Have you any ice cream cones?" Janey asked.

"Plenty!" the man replied. "What flavor?"

"Strawberry!" Janey said. "Chocolate!" cried Johnny. "Maple!" Gran'ma said. "Peach!" said Gran'pa.

"Dear me! I haven't any of those flavors! I never heard of them!" And the man leaned upon the counter and scratched his head.

"Never heard of chocolate!" exclaimed Johnny.

"What flavors have you?" asked Janey.

"I have Plumpdoodle, Wiggledoos, Kneebud and Lop-jiggle!"

"Let me try a Lopjiggle!" said Janey.

"Plumpdoodle!" Gran'ma decided.

"Wiggledoos!" cried Johnny. "They must be fine!"

"I believe I will have a Kneebud!" said Gran'pa.

The man handed out the different ice cream cones, and although the flavor of each was different from anything they had ever tasted the travelers thought them fine.

Just then the little bell up on the side of the cliff began tinkling.

"Hello!" said the man. "Someone else gets a cigar!"

They all ran to where they could look down into the little valley and there they saw old Jingles, the wicked Magician, holding on to the electric wire and turning flip-flops in his efforts to get free.

The Soft-Voiced Cow began switching her tail nervously.

"It's Old Jingles, the Magician!" cried all in one voice.

"I have been in hopes I should land him on the wire!" said the man. "Do you know," he explained in a confidential tone, "that is the reason I started this place in the mountains! Here, Gran'pa," he continued, "you may have his cigar. All of you help yourselves to anything you wish. I am through with the business now that old Jingles is on the wire!"

"What do you intend doing?" asked Gran'pa.

"Nothing," answered the man. "I'm through now, and I'm going back to the City of Nite!"

The bell kept on tinkling and the indicator on the dial kept whirling around in a circle.

"Take all the cigars you wish!" the man called to Johnny and Janey, who were behind the counter. "He's ringing up quite a lot!"

"I am glad your wire stopped the wicked creature," said Gran'ma, "for he was after us and would soon have overtaken us. He took the children's Flying Machine and he took Gran'pa's Flying Boat, and he is the one who put the Princess of Nite into the Green Jar!"

"Put the lovely Princess in the Green Jar!" the man exclaimed.

"Yes!" Gran'pa answered, as they stood and watched the antics of the Magician. "And Gran'ma rescued her! The Princess is on her way to the City of Nite now, in the Dancing Master's Umbrella!"

"Not Tiptoe's Magic Umbrella?" the man asked, in surprise.

"Yes," answered Gran'pa. "His name is Tiptoe and he was the Princess' Dancing Master."

"And my brother!" said the Little Man.

"Sh!" he added in a whisper, as he glanced hastily about as if to see that no others were listening. "It's a secret! I was the Chief of Detectives in the City of Nite when the Princess disappeared, and I had to leave when I found out that the wicked creature who claimed to be the Princess really was a Witch! She made it so unpleasant for me that I decided to go in search of Old Jingles the Magician, to see if he would help me find the real Princess. Excuse me a moment," and he went back of the counter where the children were eating the strange ice creams with large spoons.

Opening a box with a key which he wore on his watch chain, he studied the figures on a number of dials; then when he had written the figures upon a piece of paper, he handed it to Johnny.

"Can you add?" he asked.

Johnny ran his eyes over the figures. "Nine hundred and fifty-eight!" he said, as he returned the paper to the Chief of Detectives.

"Not half enough!" said the Chief of Detectives, as he pulled six little levers. There was a steady buzz-buzz that grew louder and louder every minute.

Johnny watched the hands on the dials climb and climb.

"Fifteen hundred and ninety-eight!" he cried out, presently.

"That's better!" said the Chief of Detectives. "Give the Soft-Voiced Cow some of that pop-corn in the green box; it has no mustard on it!"

"He's hopping to beat the band!" Gran'ma cried delightedly, as the Chief of Detectives came up to where they were watching the Magician.

"I should think he would!" said the man. "I turned on the current twice as hard!"

Just then they saw the Dancing Master coming over the hill into the valley.

"Here he comes now!" cried Gran'pa. "It's your brother, Tiptoe!"

"All stay here!" cried the Chief of Detectives. "Don't move from this spot!" And with this he set off at a good speed across the valley to meet his brother.

CHAPTER X

The Tiptoe Brothers and the Slide Raft

GRAN'MA and Gran'pa saw the Tiptoe Brothers throw their arms around each other's necks in their joy at meeting, but they walked in a wide circle around the spot where Jingles the Magician was dancing in his efforts to free himself from the wire.

"I should have been sooner," said the Dancing Master to Gran'pa and Gran'ma, "but just as I started to leave the Cottage-Cave I saw a Flying Boat coming across the country, and I knew from your story that the wicked Jingles must be in it."

"What did he do?" asked the children.

"He left his Flying Boat out in front of the Cottage-Cave and came inside, and while he was snooping around I slipped out the back way, went round the Cottage-Cave, and touched a match to his Flying Boat! He will have to walk from now on!" And the Dancing Master did a graceful little dance step and snapped his fingers.

"Oh dear!" Gran'ma cried as she sat down hard upon the grass.

"Whatever is the matter?" the Tiptoe Brothers cried, as Gran'pa helped Gran'ma to her feet.

"It was our Flying Boat!" replied Gran'pa quietly, "and the only way we had of ever getting back home to the Earth!"

The Dancing Master was crestfallen. "I am always putting my foot into it!" he exclaimed.

"Please do not worry," said Gran'ma, seeing how sorry the Dancing Master felt. "You did just what you thought was best!"

"Indeed I did!" answered the Dancing Master. "But that does not bring back the Flying Boat."

"What do you intend doing with the wicked Magician?" asked Gran'pa.

"Nothing!" replied the Chief of Detectives. "He is very well off where he is, and he will never be able to do any mischief as long as he holds on to the wire, or," he added with a sly wink at the Soft-Voiced Cow, "until the wire lets go of him!"

"I feel sorry for him!" said Janey.

"Well you need not, Sis!" Johnny cried. "Look at me and you will see about how you look! And it is all the wicked Jingles' fault!"

"Why, what in the world is the matter?" asked the Dancing Master, noticing for the first time that Janey and Johnny had grown so much taller.

"We caught hold of the wire!" replied Johnny.

"And it made you grow so much taller?" cried the Dancing Master in astonishment.

"Have they grown taller?" asked the Chief of Detectives.

"Certainly!" the Dancing Master answered. "They were only children and were no taller than myself when they left me three hours ago!"

Without saying a word, the Chief of Detectives motioned to the children and the others to follow him, and going to the counter he took a small case from under the counter, and from it a tiny bellows.

He then blew a puff of powder over the children and in a short time they had resumed their normal size.

Then, putting the case in his pocket, the Chief of Detectives said it would be best for them to try and reach the City of Nite as soon as possible.

"We shall have the old Witch to contend with when we reach there," he reminded the others, "and perhaps even now the Princess is under the power of the wicked creature!"

"Let us hasten!" cried Gran'pa.

The road now led down the mountain side. A short distance from the Chief of Detective's hut it wound through a deep forest, which made the traveling cool and comfortable.

At last they came to a section of the forest where all the trees were of pine. Here there was a thick carpet of pine needles that had dropped from the boughs for years.

They were smooth, soft and slippery.

"Let's get a board and slide down the mountain on the pine needles!" said Gran'pa, noticing that there was a clear space beneath the trees, which slanted straight down the mountain side.

"There are no boards about!" said Gran'ma.

"I'll run back to the hut up the mountain and get some!" the Chief of Detectives volunteered, and away he started.

"Wait there for me!" he called as he disappeared up the path.

The party sat down to wait the return of the Chief of Detectives.

"It was funny the electric wire did not affect the Soft-Voiced Cow!" mused Johnny. "It surely made Janey and me grow like weeds!"

"I'll ask my brother about it when he returns!" replied the Dancing Master.

It was not long before they heard the Chief of Detectives singing a yodel song, and soon he came into view over the rocks, carrying a pile of boards, a hammer, some nails and a long piece of rope.

As Gran'pa was an expert carpenter he offered to fix the sliding boards.

"Let's build one big sled!" he suggested, "and then we can all be together."

"A good idea!" agreed the Tiptoe Brothers.

So Gran'pa hammered the boards together and tied them in such a manner that soon he had a fine looking Slide Raft.

"We should have a rudder to guide it with," Gran'pa said as he stood and studied his work, "for who knows but that the mountain may take a few sudden turns farther down!"

So Gran'pa with his jack knife sawed away at a small tree until he had cut it down, and with the help of the rope and some small pieces of boards he made a rudder.

They all sat down on the Slide Raft, and with everybody pushing and shoving the Slide Raft started down the mountain side, gaining momentum as it went over the slippery needles.

The Soft-Voiced Cow sat in the center of the Slide Raft and the others about her. Gran'pa stood at the rudder to guide the Slide Raft should they come to a sudden turn.

It was well that Gran'pa had thought of the rudder, for when they had slid down the mountain for about a mile, and the Slide Raft was speeding along at a terrific pace, they came to where the open space beneath the trees turned sharply to the right.

Gran'pa swung the rudder round as hard as he could and turned the Slide Raft just in time to escape the trees at the side.

Down, down, the Slide Raft sped, until it was going so

fast that its occupants could not talk. The wind whistled past them like a gale, and if it had not been for the weight of the Soft-Voiced Cow they would have been swept from the Slide Raft by the force of the wind.

Just as they were nearing the bottom of the mountain the ground took a dip. Down this the frail Slide Raft shot suddenly, and up the other side.

Gran'ma and Janey screamed as the Slide Raft left the ground at the top of the little mound and plunged straight down for a hundred feet or more.

As good fortune had it, the path of the Slide Raft seemed to have been made for just such tobogganing. At the bottom of the fearful drop the ground fell away in a graceful curve, so, after hitting the ground at the bottom of the mountain, the Slide Raft went about five hundred feet out across a small pond at the edge of the pine forest, skipping across the water like a skipper rock thrown by a boy, and came to rest a short distance from the opposite bank.

As the Slide Raft stopped, the Soft-Voiced Cow fell over on her side and closed her eyes.

Gran'pa jumped from the raft and pulled it into shore, while the Tiptoe Brothers filled their hats with water which they dashed over the head of the Soft-Voiced Cow.

"She has fainted!" Gran'ma said.

"Let's get her ashore!" Johnny cried. "Everybody take hold!"

It took a lot of pulling and tugging, but finally they got the Soft-Voiced Cow up the bank and pulled grass for a pillow.

"I wish I had my smelling salts!" cried Gran'ma.

The water did not seem to help the Soft-Voiced Cow, and she rolled her eyes in an alarming manner.

"She may start kicking any minute!" Gran'pa warned. "Don't get too close to her heels! I had a cow that acted the same way once!"

Sure enough, the Soft-Voiced Cow did begin kicking, and as they drew away from her she turned her head towards Gran'ma with a pathetic look in her eyes.

"I'm going to hold her head!" cried Gran'ma, forgetting in her anxiety that her friend was only a Cow.

Gran'ma's soft hand smoothed the Soft-Voiced Cow's forehead, and the Cow, seeming to feel Gran'ma's affection, placed one of her front feet on Gran'ma's lap. Gran'ma sat holding the Cow's foot and smoothing her brow, meanwhile talking to her in a gentle, soothing manner.

The others, who stood by watching, had to brush the tears from their eyes.

"Why not puff your magic powder on her?" Janey cried to the Chief of Detectives.

"It will only cure magic!" cried that good little man as he took the tiny bellows from his pocket.

Johnny jumped forward and blew a generous puff upon the Soft-Voiced Cow's head.

The Soft-Voiced Cow seemed to shrink in size and turned a different color.

"Now, Mister! You *HAVE* done it!" Janey cried as she stamped her foot at Johnny.

Johnny stood as if frozen, watching the Soft-Voiced Cow.

"She's got a HAND!" Gran'ma cried excitedly. "Two of them!"

As the others drew closer they saw that their friend, the Soft-Voiced Cow, was turning into a woman.

The Tiptoe Brothers uttered glad cries, and the Dancing Master threw his arms about the woman.

"My wife!" he cried as he kissed her.

"It's Jenny!" cried the Chief of Detectives, turning a radiant face to Gran'pa.

"There! You see?" Johnny said, as he and Janey turned their backs on the reunited pair. "If the magic wire could not make the Soft-Voiced Cow grow taller it was because she already had been magicked. So I remembered that the powder cured magic, and there you are!"

"Johnny, you're a dear!" Janey answered, as she gave him a great hug. "You always know just what to do, all the time!"

"Ah, shucks!" Johnny replied. "I did it without much thinking!"

"Well, you did it, anyway!" his sister insisted. "To think she was a lady all this time and we did not know it!"

"She was a very ladylike Cow, at least!" said Johnny.

Mr. and Mrs. Tiptoe came up to Johnny and Janey and thanked them for what they had done.

"It was Johnny!" said Janey, generously, as the pretty lady kissed her.

"It was Janey who suggested it!" said Johnny as he bashfully received Mrs. Tiptoe's reward.

The happy little Dancing Master told his wife all that had happened since the Princess and she had disappeared, and that now the Princess was safe at home.

"At least, I hope she is," he added. "She left us and flew off for the City of Nite in the Magic Umbrella. Now tell us of your strange adventure!"

"There is not much to tell," Mrs. Tiptoe said, as the happy party walked over the fields. "When you left me in the rooms of the Witch she was hiding behind a door all the time, and just as you left she pushed me into the Magic Umbrella and jumped in with me. We flew out of the window.

"As you now know, it does not take the Magic Umbrella long to get where you wish it to go, or at least it did not take us long to get to where it settled to the ground. I could scarcely stand when we got there. The wicked creature struck me with her cane and said a strange rhyme, and I did not know a thing until I awakened with my head in Gran'ma's lap."

"How does it come that you are here, too?" she asked of the Chief of Detectives.

"I started to tell Gran'ma and Gran'pa up on the mountain a while ago," he replied, "but I got off the subject. Now I will tell the story, strange as it may seem."

"Here comes the Magic Umbrella!" cried Gran'ma, as she pointed to a speck in the air.

"It's the Princess!" cried the Detective. "No, it isn't, either," he added as the Magic Umbrella drew closer.

It proved to be the General of the Guard, and when he had embraced the Tiptoe Brothers and Mrs. Tiptoe he was introduced to the rest of the party.

"The Princess is quite safe!" he exclaimed, as all started to ask after her, "and she has sent me to try and find you and bring you to the Castle."

CHAPTER XI

AGAIN WE MEET THE PRINCESS, THE PALACE AND THE MAGICIAN

THE General of the Guard took a knapsack from his back and spread a large piece of silk upon the ground. Then with heavy twine, he fastened the four corners of the silk to the Magic Umbrella.

"Gran'ma, Janey and Mrs. Tiptoe, you ladies can ride in the Magic Umbrella and we men will ride underneath," he directed. And when all had taken their places, the General of the Guard told Gran'ma to wish the Magic Umbrella to fly to the Princess' Castle, and away they started.

The City of Nite was built upon a beautiful island and in the center stood the wonderful Castle, its tall spires and towers rising high above all the other buildings.

As they approached the Castle, the Magic Umbrella settled upon one of the broad terraces. The Princess came running out to meet them as the party climbed out of the Magic Umbrella.

Mrs. Tiptoe had to tell the Princess of her adventure as they went inside the Castle.

"And to think you were the Soft-Voiced Cow," laughed the Princess, "and that none of us suspected it! My, I am glad we are all safe and sound and home again!"

"We are very glad too," Gran'ma said, "but Gran'pa, Janey, Johnny and I are still very far from home!"

"Oh, you will like it here," the Princess laughed as she threw her arms about Gran'ma. "And I shall have you live here with me all the time in the Castle, for we owe everything to you!"

"You saved the Princess from the Green Jar and charmed away the wicked magic from Mrs. Tiptoe!" exclaimed the General of the Guard.

"We must keep you with us always," the Princess said as the party walked into a great hall. "Now, Gran'pa," she continued, "I will let Mr. Tiptoe show you and Johnny to your rooms, and when all have dressed we are going to have a nice little party all to ourselves. I will take Gran'ma and Janey and Mrs. Tiptoe to their rooms and we will meet you in the Banquet Hall very soon."

The Princess led Gran'ma, Janey and Mrs. Tiptoe to a wonderful room with ivory and gold beds. Beautiful draperies hung from the windows, and a merry little fountain tinkled in one corner of the room.

"Here are your clothes," the Princess said, opening a closet and displaying rows and rows of wonderful silk and satin dresses.

Janey's eyes were the size of saucers. Some of the dresses were pink—and pink was her favorite color!

"I had them all made to fit you and Janey," she told

*Gran'ma, Janey and Mrs. Tiptoe rode in the Magic Umbrella
and the men rode underneath.*

Gran'ma. "I am so sorry I did not know that Mrs. Tiptoe was to be with us, but she may have one of Janey's dresses, I'm sure!"

"Indeed she may!" Janey cried. "Oh, thank you so much, Your Majesty!"

"Now, see here!" cried the Princess, pretending to be very stern. "Do not 'Your Majesty' me! I am to be plain Nidia to all of you, so you must begin to get used to calling me that!"

When the Princess, Mrs. Tiptoe, Gran'ma and Janey reached the Banquet Hall, Gran'pa, Johnny and the Tiptoe Brothers were there waiting for them.

"Whee! How fine you all look!" Johnny cried, as he saw the beautiful silk and satin dresses.

"You look fine, too!" Janey exclaimed. "All of you!"

"How did the Princess know our measurements?" Johnny whispered to Janey as they took their seats at the table.

"I don't know," Janey replied, rather puzzled. "Just see Gran'pa! My, doesn't he look nice in that purple velvet!"

"We are very anxious to know how you got rid of the wicked Witch when you returned to the Castle," Gran'ma said to the Princess.

The Princess laughed a merry laugh and replied, "I am afraid you will be disappointed with my adventure, for when I left you upon the mountain side at Mr. Tiptoe's Cottage-Cave I wished the Magic Umbrella to take me to my mother, but as I flew over the City of Nite I changed my mind.

"'No,' I said to myself, 'I will go right to the Castle and face the wicked Witch!'

"And so I wished to go to the Castle instead of to my mother. And when I climbed out of the Magic Umbrella I ran right into the Castle and it was empty! I went through all the rooms and found no one; the wicked Witch was not there at all!"

"Did you go into the little room at the top of the Blue Tower?" Mr. Tiptoe asked. "That is where she was the day Mrs. Tiptoe and I found her."

"Yes, I went there, too," the Princess replied, "and cobwebs were all over everything. I knew the wicked creature had not been there for months."

"For years, to be more exact," interrupted the Chief of Detectives.

"How do you know?" the Princess asked the Chief of Detectives in surprise.

The Chief of Detectives explained.

"I started to tell of my adventure to Gran'ma and the

others on the mountain side," he said, "but I was so glad to see my brother coming across the meadow I forgot what I was saying."

"Tell us now! Perhaps you can clear up the mystery!" the Princess cried. "No one in the City of Nite could tell me anything! Please tell us all you know, and all about your adventure!"

"But you had not finished telling us of your own experience," the Chief of Detectives answered.

"There is very little more to tell," said the Princess. "When I discovered that the wicked Witch was not in the Castle and that she had not been here for some time, I rang the Great Bell five times. This, as you know, is the signal for every one in the City of Nite to have a holiday. And when the good people heard the Great Bell pealing, they came running to the Castle and found me! That is all there is to tell, except that every thing inside the Castle had grown dreadfully musty, so I had everything cleaned, and new draperies and then I sent the General of the Guard in the Magic Umbrella to bring you here."

When the Princess had finished the Chief of Detectives told his story.

"When the Princess disappeared," he began, "I was away on my vacation and word did not reach me for four days. But you may rest assured that when I did hear I hurried back to the City of Nite as fast as possible.

"I asked everyone I met about the strange disappearance of the Princess, for I could not believe that the Princess had been changed into an old woman. No one could help me. People just stood around looking at one another as if they were stunned. At first I thought it unwise to visit this old Witch for fear she might find out that I distrusted her, but upon second thought I changed my plans and went to see her."

"I suppose I may tell our good friends of the secret passage?" the Chief of Detectives interrupted himself to ask the Princess, and being given permission he went on:

"There are secret passages built in the walls of the Castle which lead to many of the rooms, and by which anyone who knows how to open the secret doors may escape. Now I, of course, knew all the doors and all the buttons that open them, so I went through all the secret passages and from their peep-holes I looked into all the rooms. But I could never time my visits just right until about a year ago.

"Then one day as I walked through one of the secret passages, I heard someone talking, so I hastily glued my eyes to the peephole, you may be sure. But when I looked through, I did not see the Witch in the room! Instead, there stood a queer man with a tall hat and a crooked stick.

"I could not quite make out what he was saying, for he was only talking to himself and at times merely mumbled his words, but I learned enough to know that he had no business there."

"Jingles the Magician!" cried the Princess, Gran'ma and Janey in one breath.

"You are right," continued the Chief of Detectives. "I heard him mutter something about a book of rhymes, and he played with a queer little pouch with tassels!"

"The Magic Whistle!" cried Gran'pa and Johnny.

"I don't know what it was," said the Chief of Detectives. "But as I watched the queer man he took off his tall hat and coat and put them in a closet; then he took out a white wig and a great cloak and bonnet and put them on. I saw then that he and the Witch were one and the same and I knew positively that neither was our beloved Princess. I did not know what to do! At first I thought of calling the people together and telling them of what I had seen, but then, thought I, 'Should I do that, I may never discover what has become of the Princess.'

"So I watched at the secret passage for days and days until once again I was rewarded. There was the queer man again, sitting and reading a large book and trying to memorize some verses. Then I watched him until I saw him put on a pair of spectacles. He stared for a moment for all the world like a near-sighted person. Then he skipped up and down.

"'Someone is drinking my lemonade,' he cried, looking through them. 'Hooray! Now I will have someone else to work my magic on!' And with this, he jumped upon his large book and flew right out of the window!"

"It was Janey who drank at the lemonade spring!" cried Johnny.

"I did not know that, of course," said the Chief of Detectives. "However, when the wicked man left, I went into the room and looked about. In the pocket of the cloak which the Witch had worn, I discovered the tiny powder puff which Johnny puffed upon the Soft Voiced Cow, or upon Mrs. Tiptoe, I should have said! I also found a tiny book of magic and a few brass buttons and other charms.

"I took the powder puff, the tiny book of magic and the charms; I also made a drawing of the queer designs upon the floor. Then I left everything else just as I had found it and went home.

"I studied the book of magic a long time before I finally tested out some magic myself. First, I copied the designs upon a large white rug then, following the directions in the little book, I placed the charms about as directed, then I puffed a bit of powder into a tin cup and touched a match to it. When the powder puffed up into the room, I went out of the door as fast as I could. But when I saw the room had cleared, I ventured back and found written upon the slate—I forgot to mention that one of the things called for in the book was a slate and pencil—'Top of Whippoorwill Mountain. Electric wires strung meadow. Capture!'

"I puzzled and puzzled over this message, and I tried the magic three times. The same message always came upon the slate! Then I decided to go to the top of Whippoorwill Mountain and see the wires, but there were no wires there!

"'Perhaps it means that I am to put the wires there,' I thought. 'At least I can try it!' So I had the Royal Electrician fix up the wires about the meadow, and then I built the little hut and filled it with ice cream and pop corn and cigars, so that if I accidentally caught any innocent persons, I could give them candy cigars and pop corn and ice cream. And right there I stayed until, as you know, I caught old Jingles."

"You have caught old Jingles the Magician!" cried the Princess.

"Yes," Gran'ma laughed, "and he also caught Janey and Johnny and the Soft-Voiced Cow and myself!"

"I had forgotten the Princess did not know that I had caught the wicked creature and that we left him jumping to beat the band and hanging on to the electric wire," the Chief of Detectives said. Then, turning to the Princess, he continued, "I was careful to turn on the current so that he would have a good dose too!"

"I am truly glad we have all escaped from him," the Princess said and as all had finished eating by this time she asked Gran'ma, "How would you like to ride about the City of Nite and see the sights?"

"Oh, let's do!" Gran'ma cried, jumping up. "I have always wanted to go to a City and we never felt we had enough money to do so when we were upon the Earth!"

"Well, you will find everything in the City of Nite free to all of you," laughed the Princess, "for everyone knows all about you and what you have done for us, so if you are all of the same mind we can start right now."

"Let's walk!" said Gran'ma, when the Princess said something about carriages. "Then we can all be together and look in the shop windows and have lots more fun!"

"I often walk about the town, or at least, I used to walk about, before I was put in the Green Jar," the Princess replied.

"It's nice to get up from the table and not have to worry about doing the dishes," said Gran'ma. "Let's start right away Gran'pa, you'll have to buy a bag of peanuts apiece. We always have peanuts when we go to town," she explained to the Princess.

"Had we better take an umbrella?" asked Gran'pa. "One usually carries an umbrella when one goes to town. It might rain."

"Perhaps it would be as well to take the Magic Umbrella with us," the Princess laughed, although she could not understand just why Gran'pa should wish to carry one, for it very seldom rained in the beautiful City.

So the happy visitors walked down the great steps of the Castle with the Princess and her old friends and into the

shopping center of the City of Nite, where all the kindly faced people bowed to them all as they passed.

The Princess stopped and talked with the people and gave presents to the little children whom they met.

At the first store they came to Gran'pa tried to buy some peanuts, but the shopkeeper would not accept anything for them.

"You couldn't pay anyhow," Johnny laughed. "You haven't any Moon money, it's all Earth money in your purse."

"To be sure it is," Gran'pa replied. "I had forgotten that!"

The Princess took them into all the ice cream parlors and candy stores in the City, and when they returned to the Castle all were loaded with bundles.

As they neared the steps of the Castle, Gran'pa shouted, "Look at the crowd near the Castle door. "It must be people who have come to see you about something!"

The Princess looked worried. "No," she replied, "they would never crowd about the Castle door in such a disorderly manner. Something has happened!"

Just as they started up the long flight of steps, the crowd separated and as the people fell back on either side a tall form dashed out of the doorway waving his crooked stick and shouting hoarsely.

"Old Jingles, the Magician!" the Princess cried as she sank to the steps.

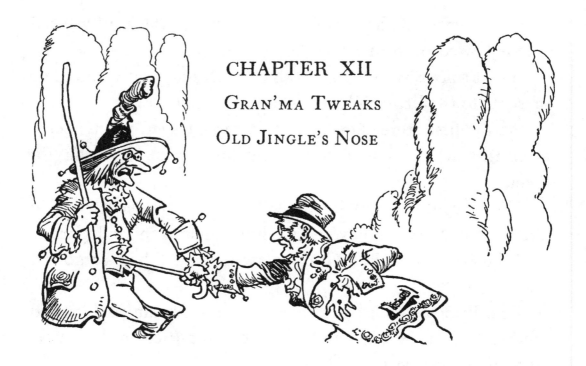

CHAPTER XII

GRAN'MA TWEAKS

OLD JINGLE'S NOSE

G RAN'MA, Janey and Mrs. Tiptoe rushed to the Princess and, raising her between them, they half carried and half dragged her back down the marble steps.

The Chief of Detectives, the Dancing Master, Johnny and Gran'pa sprang up the steps to meet the Magician. But the Chief of Detectives and Johnny caught their feet together and went tumbling to the foot of the hard stone steps, where they lay dazed.

The Dancing Master, who was very active, sprang up the steps two at a time and met the Magician on the broad landing and attacked him, although he scarcely reached to the Magician's waist.

Old Jingles struck at the Dancing Master with his cane, but the Dancing Master dodged in under the blow and grappled with the Magician.

The good people of Nite were terror stricken, and stood motionless as the two struggled together.

Finally the Magician pulled his tiny bellows from his pocket and blew it toward the Dancing Master's back, and the Dancing Master fell to the steps, just as Gran'pa struck the bellows from the Magician's hand with his cane.

With a roar of pain and rage the wicked Jingles swung his crooked stick at Gran'pa's head. Gran'pa warded off the blow with his own polished cane and, using it as a sword, he jabbed old Jingles in the stomach.

The Magician swung his large crooked stick again, and Gran'pa again poked him in the stomach, and then, as the wicked creature backed away, Gran'pa gave him a smart tap on the head, sending his tall hat spinning down the steps.

The Princess had recovered and was watching the duel with fascination. Gran'ma was struggling between Janey and Mrs. Tiptoe.

"Let me go!" she cried. "Let me get to him! I'll tweak his nose! He sha'n't hurt Gran'pa! Let me go!"

But Janey and Mrs. Tiptoe held her and tried to watch at the same time.

"Why don't the people help?" Gran'ma cried. "Let me go, I tell you! I'll show him, the wicked old thing!"

[143]

Gran'pa had just swung his cane at the Magician's head again hoping to finish him with one more blow, but the Magician stepped to one side and struck Gran'pa on the head, sending him to his knees. Gran'pa, however much the blow hurt, never uttered a groan, and as he struggled dizzily to his feet he tried to ward off the blows that old Jingles showered upon him.

Part of the blows Gran'pa received on his left arm, the others slid harmlessly off his cane.

Gran'pa backed away from the Magician and his face was worried, for the blow upon his head had made Gran'pa weak in the knees.

But although he dodged and gave ground Gran'pa waited for an opening and at last, as the Magician missed a swing at Gran'pa's head, Gran'pa drew his cane back over his shoulder and brought it down with all his might upon old Jingles' crown.

The blow was of such force it would have broken the Magician's head if the cane had not split in two, and as it was the wicked man staggered from the blow.

Gran'pa, with but the handle of his cane in his hand, jumped forward to strike again, but he missed his footing and went rolling down the stone steps.

When Gran'pa fell in front of the Magician, the Princess, Janey and Mrs. Tiptoe started running.

"Run for your lives!" cried the Princess. "He will change all of us into animals! Run!"

The Magician staggered after Gran'pa who had rolled clear to the bottom of the long flight of steps. The Magician in his anger did not see Johnny or the Chief of Detectives, who still sat in a daze part of the way down the steps, so as he passed them, Johnny stuck his foot out and tripped up the Magician.

Down the long flight of steps the Magician fell, his long arms and legs hitting the steps and his crooked stick flying high in the air as he turned over and over.

Johnny, though still dazed, got to his feet and started down the steps, hoping he could get the Magician's crooked stick.

The Magician rolled to the bottom of the steps and he found Gran'ma there to meet him; for as soon as the others had started to run, they had released Gran'ma.

So Gran'ma waited until old Jingles had stopped rolling, then she rushed at him, and, catching his long nose in her hands, she gave it a tweak.

With one scream of pain, the Magician lay still, and as Johnny raised the crooked stick to bring it down upon Jingles' head, Gran'ma stopped him.

"I said I'd tweak his nose," Gran'ma cried, "and I'll tweak it again just as soon as he awakens!"

Gran'pa sat up and looked around.

"Give me another sack of peanuts," he said.

The Magician showed signs of awakening, so Gran'ma gave his long nose another tweak which made him lie still.

The Princess called to the people still standing around the door of the Castle.

"Call the Guards!" she shouted. "We'll tie him and keep him chained up for ever!"

The voice of their Princess seemed to arouse the people from their numbness and fear and eight Guards came running out from behind the great doors where they had hidden themselves.

When the Guards came to pick up the Magician to carry him away Gran'ma pushed them back.

"No you don't!" she told them. "He stays right here while I tweak his nose until he never has another speck of magic in him!"

And as the Magician stirred again, Gran'ma gave his long nose another hard tweak.

"But Gran'ma," Janey cried, "the Princess must be obeyed! She wants the wicked creature put in chains and in prison!"

"Now, you let me be!" Gran'ma said. "I'm boss here and here he stays until I—"

Just as this moment the Dancing Master rushed down the steps and blew a puff from the magic bellows upon the face of old Jingles. It first formed a puffy white cloud, then it settled grain by grain. There was a breathless silence.

Gran'ma did not finish what she was about to say, for as the magic powder touched the Magician's face, his long nose disappeared, his wicked eyes changed and his face took on the appearance of a young man. And as they all watched in won-

Catching his long nose in her hands she gave it a tweak.

der and amazement they saw his long, thin fingers change into young hands, and the thin form beneath the torn, dusty clothes alter until a fine young man lay before them.

The Dancing Master blew another puff of the powder upon the prostrate form and the old torn clothes changed into silk and velvet.

"Dear me!" Gran'ma cried. "Perhaps we have made a mistake! It isn't old Jingles!"

And when the Strange Young Man opened his eyes and saw the crowd standing around him, he ran his hand across his forehead as if trying to recollect something.

"Where am I?" he asked.

"You are in the City of Nite," answered the Princess. "Guards, assist him into the Castle!"

"I believe I can walk," said the Strange Young Man, "but I cannot imagine how I got here, for I have never heard of the City of Nite before." And with this he stood upon his feet.

"This is indeed strange," said the Princess. "Let us all go into the Castle." And as the people drew aside to let them pass, the Princess, Mrs. Tiptoe, Gran'ma and Janey went up the steps, followed by the Strange Young Man, the Tiptoe Brothers, Gran'pa and Johnny.

"My name is David," the Strange Young Man said, when all had taken chairs in the Princess' drawing room and he saw that they looked to him for an explanation, "and my home is in Dayland, or at least," he continued, "it used to be there."

"Dayland is on the other side of the Moon!" said the Princess. "My father and mother and I visited there once!"

"If Dayland is on the other side of the Moon," said David, "this must be the Land Back of the Moon."

"It is," the Princess replied. "If you looked through the Moon you would see it. It's the Magical Land of Noom."

"How strange that I should be here!" and David passed his hand over his forehead in a puzzled manner. "I faintly remember strange rhymes and jingles of which I dreamed."

"You did not dream them," Gran'ma hastened to explain. "You were old Jingles the Magician until a few moments ago, then Mr. Tiptoe puffed the magic powder on you and changed you back to your own self."

"Dear me," sighed David. "If this is true tell me how long I have been in this strange shape, for I speak truly when I tell you that I am really at a loss to account for the cruel and wicked things which I must have done while I was not myself."

"You first came to the City of Nite as a witch and said you were the Princess," the Chief of Detectives told him.

"But you will remember," the Princess said, turning to the Chief of Detectives, "that I met him first as Old Jingles, when I saw the Queer Horse who had eaten his head off, and that was over eighty years ago."

"Dear me," David sighed. "Then there is no telling how long I have been old Jingles or the Witch. I'm awfully sorry," he told the Princess. "I wouldn't have harmed you for the world."

"Isn't it just like a fairy tale!" Janey cried.

"Perhaps it is," David smiled, "but it seems like a disagreeable dream to me and until I get back to my own country, I really cannot explain how it all came about."

"What is the last thing you remember?" Johnny asked.

"Let me see! We were having a great ball or something at the Castle and I had just stepped outside the door to look at the Sun when — when — well, that is the last thing I can recall, except the queer dreams about rhymes and jingles."

"You don't remember what you did with our Flying Boat, do you?" Johnny asked.

"No, I can not recall a Flying Boat, at all," David answered.

"That was the only way we had of returning to the Earth," Gran'ma said, a little sadly, "and I feel that we should return as soon as we can."

When Gran'pa had told him of the children's Flying Boat and how he had made one to follow the children to the Moon, David said, "Perhaps you could make another and so return to the Earth! Perhaps you could take me to my home in it, first."

Gran'pa asked the Princess if he could build another Flying Boat and although the Princess wished them to stay at the Castle with her always, she realized that they must be as anxious to return to the Earth as she had been to return to the City of Nite. So the Princess sent word to the Royal Carpenter to bring boards and nails to the Castle roof and there Gran'pa superintended the building of the new Flying Boat.

While this was being built, the Princess took her friends to visit her father and mother, with whom they spent two happy weeks, seeing the sights and having dances and dinners given in their honor.

When they returned to the City of Nite, the Flying Boat had been completed and stood upon the Castle roof all ready to sail. It was a sturdy, beautifully built machine—quite the nicest one that has ever been made.

There were tears in the eyes of the Princess and Mrs. Tiptoe as David, Gran'ma, Gran'pa and the children took their seats in the boat.

"Good-bye! Good-bye!" they cried. "Do not forget that we shall be most happy to have you visit us again!" And the Princess gave Gran'ma, Gran'pa, Janey and Johnny each a beautiful ring in which was set a wonderful Moonstone.

Then when she had kissed them all good-bye again Gran'pa turned the little knob marked "Start" and the new Flying Boat rose slowly from the roof of the Castle and sailed away.

The Princess and the people of Nite watched the Flying Boat until it was out of sight, and then the Princess and Mrs. Tiptoe and the Tiptoe Brothers went into the Castle.

"I wished for them to stay," said the Princess. "Didn't you love them all?"

"Indeed I did," Mrs. Tiptoe answered as she wiped her eyes. "They were all so kind and unselfish."

"It is nice to know and love them," said Mr. Tiptoe, "and while I know they had many unpleasant experiences in the Magical Land of Noom, I am so glad they came."

"Yes," replied the Princess, "we owe all our present happiness to them and I hope they will come again to visit us soon."

"Let's all write a long letter and send it to them," the Chief of Detectives suggested.

"How?" the others inquired.

"Let us write the letter, then address it care of the Earth and puff the magic powder upon it. They will be sure to receive it!"

"That is an excellent idea!" the Princess cried joyfully. "We will start it right away."

So they all set to work on the letter, so as to send it off at once.

CHAPTER XIII

Everybody Goes Home

WHEN the Flying Boat was out of sight of the City of Nite, Gran'pa pressed the speed button and the new craft shot through the air like a comet, passing over the mountains and valleys in a flash. In a very few moments it had covered a distance that had taken the travelers long hours to walk.

The new Flying Boat whizzed around the bend in the Moon and flew over the side which is always turned towards the Earth.

"This must be the Dayland in which you live!" Gran'pa said to David.

"It is!" David answered. "See, there is the Earth!"

By shading their eyes from the Sun, Gran'ma, Gran'pa and the children could see a blue-green Star winking and blinking in the sky and could faintly make out the shape of the land and the oceans upon its surface.

As they sped along above the Moon, they watched the wonderful changes in coloring below them. They saw many cities and villages and looked into enormous craters of extinct volcanoes.

At last they saw in the distance a city of white with wonderful steeples and towers on the great building standing in the center. It was a regular fairy book castle with glistening windows and hanging gardens.

"There it is!" David shouted. "Guide the Flying Boat to the balcony at the right of the Palace!" And as Gran'pa brought the Flying Boat to rest as directed, many people rushed out of the Palace, and knelt before David. "Our King has returned!" they shouted. "Long live the King!" And they all came and kissed his hand.

When David saw Gran'ma and Gran'pa and Janey and Johnny looking at him in astonishment he put his arms around them and helped them from the boat.

"We did not know you were a King!" exclaimed Janey.

The King laughed for the first time and it was such a cheery, pleasant laugh they almost forgot that he was a King and Gran'ma gave his hand a squeeze.

"There it is!" David shouted. "Guide the Flying Boat
to the balcony at the right of the Palace!"

As the King led them inside the Palace all the bells in the city began chiming. "You must at least stay and have dinner with me," he said.

The King wished them to stay until he had learned how he came to change characters, but as soon as they had finished dinner, Gran'ma said they must leave.

"If I can discover just what happened when I walked out to look at the Sun," the King laughed as he said good-bye, "I will write to you and try to find a way to get the letter into your hands."

"It seems as if you could make a little Flying Boat and put the letter in it and send it to us," Johnny said.

"Then you can expect to hear from me," the King replied, as he waved good-bye to them.

Gran'ma and the children took a nap while Gran'pa guided the Flying Boat on its return trip and when he finally awakened them, the new Flying Boat stood in the back yard near the kitchen door at Gran'pa's home.

"Well," said Gran'ma as she jumped out of the boat, "the Castle of the Princess was comfortable and beautiful and King David's Palace was magnificent, but our little old home is the best of all!"

"Be it ever so humble, there's no place like home!" Gran'pa sang as he helped Janey from the boat.

"I hope the moths haven't got in the carpets!" Gran'ma said, as she opened the back door.

Johnny ran to the chicken shed and came back with six or seven eggs.

Janey helped Gran'ma set the table and Gran'pa built the kitchen fire. Then Gran'pa went to the smoke-house and brought in a large ham.

"We'll have some good old ham and eggs!" he said.

Gran'ma made the fluffiest biscuits she had ever baked and they sat down to a breakfast which they all enjoyed more than they had ever enjoyed a breakfast before.

"Now that we are back home again, doesn't it all seem far away and strange, like a fairy tale one has read a long time ago?" Gran'ma suggested.

"Yes, and like a real fairy tale, it has turned out very happily," Gran'pa smiled.

"I wonder if we shall ever hear from the Princess or from the King," Johnny said.

"Wouldn't it be wonderful if the King should marry the beautiful Princess, just as all pretty fairy tales end?" mused Gran'ma.

THE END

CPSIA information can be obtained
at www.ICGtesting.com
Printed in the USA
BVHW061404241120
593995BV00002B/52

9 781626 549845